Umbrella Summer

Lisa Graff

LAURA GERINGER BOOKS

An Imprint of HarperCollins*Publishers*

Also by Lisa Graff:

THE LIFE AND CRIMES OF BERNETTA WALLFLOWER

THE THING ABOUT GEORGIE

Library of Congress Cataloging-in-Publication Data
Graff, Lisa (Lisa Colleen), date
Umbrella summer / Lisa Graff. — 1st ed.
  p. cm.
"Laura Geringer Books."
Summary: After her brother Jared dies, ten-year-old Annie worries about
the hidden dangers of everything, from bug bites to bicycle riding, until she
is befriended by a new neighbor who is grieving her own loss.
 ISBN 978-0-06-143189-0
 [1. Death—Fiction. 2. Grief—Fiction. 3. Worry—Fiction.] I. Title.
PZ7.G751577 Um 2009   2008026015
[Fic]—dc22   CIP
                                                             AC

Typography by Carla Weise
11 12 13 14 15   CG/CW   10 9 8 7 6 5 4
❖
First paperback edition, 2011

To Ryan

one
●●●

If you started to squeeze your brakes right in the middle of heading down Maple Hill, just as you were passing old Mr. Normore's mailbox, you could coast into the bike rack in front of Lippy's Market without making a single tire squeak. That was the fastest way to go, and the most fun too, with the wind whistling past your ears and your stomach getting fluttery and floaty, till you thought maybe you were riding quicker than a rocket.

I didn't do that anymore, though. Now I hopped off my bike at the top of the hill and walked it. It took five times as long but it was lots safer.

I got to the store at 7:58—that's what it said on the clock inside. The door was still locked, and Mr. Lippowitz and his son, Tommy, were flattening cardboard boxes in the corner. Mr. L. saw me peeking through the window and held up two fingers, so I sat down on the front step and waited, trying to soak up the whole two minutes by taking off all my biking gear real slow. I slid off my elbow pads—left one first, then the right—and stacked them on the step next to me in a pile. Next came the kneepads, which I tugged off over my sneakers, and last of all I unsnapped my bike helmet. I thought about taking off the ace bandages around my ankles, too, but then I decided it would take too long to put them back on when I was ready to bike home, and there was no way I was biking without them. They were important for protecting against sprains.

I took so long with my bike gear, I swear Mr. L. could've opened the store twice by the time I was done, but the door was still closed. I stood up and leaned back on my heels and then forward to the tippy-tips of my toes, just for something to do while I was waiting, and I scanned the bulletin board out front to see if there was anything new.

Same as usual, there were papers pinned up all over—advertisements and lost-and-founds, flyers about art lessons and people selling furniture and high school kids looking for babysitting jobs. In the top right corner there was a green one that said YARD SALE SATURDAY—106 KNICKERBOCKER LANE, and I knew that had to be the Harpers next door, because my house was 108. Some of the flyers were brand-new, and some were so old they were brown around the edges from too much sun. My dad once said that if you ever wanted to know what people were up to in Cedar Haven, California, the easiest way was to go down to Lippy's, because then you could learn about everyone all at once.

By the time Mr. L. unlocked the door, it was 8:09, but I didn't tell him that. "Well, if it isn't my best customer!" he said with a grin. "How are you doing today, Annie?"

"Pretty good," I told him. "I checked our house for

black widow spiders, and there aren't any."

"Well." His nostrils flared at that. "Good to know."

There was a crash from the back room—not an emergency-sounding shatter like plates breaking, but more like a good long rattle.

"Tommy!" Mr. L. hollered over his shoulder. "What was that?"

Tommy didn't answer.

"Sounded like a whole carton of Good & Plentys to me," I said.

He laughed. "I better go check, huh?"

While Mr. L. checked on Tommy, I wandered around. I knew exactly what I was looking for, but I liked exploring. Lippy's was one of my favorite places to be. Sometimes on Sundays, after Rebecca's family got back from church, we rode our bikes down to get lunch from the warmer. Rebecca got either fried chicken or spiced potato wedges, and I always got beef taquitos. It was four for two dollars, but if Mr. L. was at the register I got a fifth one for free.

I saw right away that Mr. L. had finally stocked up

the toy aisle for summer—water balloons and Super Soakers, snorkel masks and plastic sunglasses. He should've gotten that stuff out three weeks ago, because it was already the first day of July and I was sweating worse than a pig in a roller derby. But I guess better late than never, that's what my mom always said. There was a pair of brown-and-pink polka-dotted flip-flops that were just my size, and I wanted them real bad, but there were more important things I needed to spend my money on.

After I finished my wandering, I went to the front, where Mr. L. was reading the newspaper behind the counter.

"Was it Good & Plentys?" I asked him. "Is that what crashed?"

He shook his head. "Junior Mints. You find something worth buying today, Annie?"

"Yup." I slapped my purchase on the counter.

Mr. L. looked at the box and then looked back at me. His face was squinty. "Didn't you just buy a box of Band-Aids yesterday?" he asked.

"It was Thursday," I told him, "and I'm out already."

I saw him looking at my arms. I had two Band-Aids on the right one, where Rebecca's hamster had scratched me with its nails, and five on the left one, covering up spots that were either mosquito bites or poison oak, I wasn't sure yet.

He sighed deep. He was looking at me with his eyes big and sad, and a crease between the eyebrows. It was the same look almost everyone had for me now, Miss Kimball at school, my parents' friends, even Rebecca sometimes when she thought I couldn't see her. Everybody on the planet practically had been looking at me the same way since February—sad and worrying, with a bit of pity mixed in at the edges. I guess that was the way people looked at you after your brother died.

I slipped three dollars across the counter toward him. "I get seventeen cents change," I said.

Mr. L. just nodded and rang me up.

When I was outside trying to yank my kneepads back up around my knees, I noticed Tommy by the Dumpster. He was gnawing on a handful of Junior Mints.

Tommy had never really talked much, but it seemed to me he talked less than normal lately. I liked hanging out with him though, even if he was two years older, because he was the one person who never gave me that dead-brother look. I guess that's because he'd been Jared's best friend, so he probably had people giving him enough dead-best-friend looks to know better.

He must've seen me staring, because he held up the box of candy. It had a rip in the corner. "They got damaged," he said.

I shrugged. "Can I have some?"

He shrugged back. "Guess so."

I yanked my right kneepad up one more inch and went over to the Dumpster. Tommy shook some Junior Mints into my hand. He was eating his quick back-to-back, but I sucked on mine slow, until the chocolate melted away and all that was left was peppermint. We stood in the parking lot and chewed and sucked for a long time, just quiet. I tried to look at Tommy sideways without him noticing while I rolled a new piece of candy around on my tongue. He had blond hair that was the length my mom called "shaggy," and it covered up his whole eyebrows. That would've driven me nuts, but Tommy didn't seem to mind.

I was thinking about that when Tommy popped another Junior Mint into his mouth and said, "We were gonna go bowling this year."

I nodded. Jared and Tommy had their birthday party together every year, since they were born only two days apart, July seventh for Tommy and the ninth for Jared. They either went to Castle Park, where they had miniature golf and video games, or else they went bowling. I liked bowling better because I always had to come, and when it came to video games I stunk worse than old asparagus.

"You still gonna go?" I asked him. I plucked another Junior Mint from my hand and let the chocolate settle onto the top of my tongue.

He shook out the last of the candy into his mouth. "Maybe. I guess." He tossed the empty box into the Dumpster. "I don't know."

He was about to go back inside the store, I could tell,

but for some reason I didn't want him to leave just yet.

"Tommy?" I said.

He turned around. "Yeah?"

Then I realized I shouldn't have said "Tommy?" with the question-mark sound in my voice, because that made it sound like I had a question to ask him, which I didn't. So then I had to think of one. "Um, if you were writing a will, what do you think you'd put in there?"

Tommy raised an eyebrow. "A will?"

"Yeah," I said. "Like, when someone dies and they leave you stuff." I hadn't been planning to talk to Tommy about wills. But I'd been thinking about them for a while, how they were good to have around for just-in-case times. If Jared had made one, I was pretty sure he would've given his robot collection to me, so it wouldn't just sit shut up inside his bedroom where Mom said it should be. "What would you write?"

Tommy still had his eyebrow up. It was a look Jared sometimes used to have when he talked to me, that look that meant he couldn't believe he was related to someone so stupid. Usually after a look like that, Jared gave me a wet willy and told me to stop being a moron, but Tommy just said, "What do you mean, what would I write?"

"Like, what sort of stuff would you give away, and to who?"

He was quiet for a while, thinking I guess, and I sucked on my last Junior Mint until it was just peppermint air.

"I don't know," he said at last. He shrugged when he said it. "Probably no one wants any of my stuff anyway." He squinted at me from under his shaggy hair. "Why do you want to know?"

I tapped the Band-Aid box bulge in my front pocket. "I've been thinking about writing one," I said. "But I can't figure out who should get which things." Like my stuffed turtle Chirpy, the one Jared gave me for my birthday three years ago, and my snow globe from Death Valley. Should I leave that stuff to my parents? Rebecca? The Goodwill box at school? It was hard to figure out.

"Okay, well"—Tommy did head for the door then—
"good luck." And I knew that meant we were done
talking. I finished putting on the rest of my bike gear,
checked three times to make sure my shoelaces were
double-knotted, and then whacked up my kickstand.

The whole way home, with the corner of the Band-
Aid box poking into my hip as I walked my bike slowly
up Maple Hill, I thought about it. My will. The best
thing to do would be to make one as soon as possible,
because you never knew when you were going to need
it, and it was best to be prepared. But the reason I was
having problems was because most of the stuff I had, if
I could give it to anyone, I'd want to give it to Jared.

And Jared was gone.

two
●●●

When I got home, I sat down on the porch steps to change one of my Band-Aids, because the edges were looking kind of grimy. Then I noticed some bumps on my left leg, just above the knee. There were two of them, red and itchy, and they looked like bug bites, but I checked all over to make sure there weren't more of them, because that could mean they were chicken pox. I'd never had that one before, and there'd been a boy at the library last week who looked pretty itchy. I'd told Mom the kid seemed chicken poxy right when I saw him, but she just rolled her eyes.

Mom was always saying I shouldn't worry so much, but I knew for a fact that she didn't worry enough. Because last February when Jared got hit with a hockey puck playing out on Cedar Lake, Mom took him to the hospital, and the doctor said he just had chest pain from where the puck had hit him, and Mom believed it. And then two days later, Jared died. There was a problem with his heart. The doctors at the hospital said it was incredibly rare, that's why no one had thought to check for it. But rare didn't matter for Jared, did it?

The problem was, you couldn't just look out for the big things—cars on the highway and stinging jellyfish and getting hit by lightning and house fires and pneumonia. Everyone knew that stuff was dangerous. But there was a lot of other dangerous stuff that most people didn't even think to worry about. You had to watch out for everything.

I was checking underneath my sock for more red bumps when a head popped up on the other side of the hedge and scared me so bad, I lost my balance and fell right over in the grass.

"Why, hello there, Annie! Oh, I'm so sorry, dear, I didn't mean to startle you."

It was Mrs. Harper, our next-door neighbor, who did not normally scare the bejeebers out of me.

"That's okay," I told her. I stood up and patted all my bones to make sure none of them were broken. They weren't. "I'm all right."

"Glad to hear it," she said.

Mrs. Harper was a fairly large lady, as big around as one and a half of most people, and she liked giving hugs. Every time she saw you, she'd squeeze you up tight into a hug and hold on to you so long that you could sing the whole "Star-Spangled Banner" before she was done. She was our troop leader for Junior Sunbirds, so every meeting the hugs could go on forever. "What are you up to over here?"

"Just checking to make sure I don't have chicken pox," I told her, brushing the grass off me.

"Oh." Mrs. Harper cleared her throat then, even though I could tell it didn't really need clearing. "I see. Well"—she cleared her throat again—"anyway, Mr.

14
● ● ●

Harper and I are having a yard sale today. Would you like to come over and take a look? We have some of the kids' old toys and things."

I peered over the hedge into their yard, and sure enough, there was Mr. Harper, arranging a pile of old mugs on a fold-out table. There were tables all over the yard, actually, but I couldn't tell what was on most of them. A couple of people from our neighborhood were already wandering around looking at things. "I don't have any money," I said.

Mrs. Harper nodded. "Well, how about this then? Why don't you come be our helper? You can help Mr. Harper and me watch the tables and count money, and then you can pick out one thing to keep, anything you want."

I thought about it. If I went over there, she was going to hug me for sure. But there might be some good loot on those tables. Like one of those mats with the bumps to make sure you didn't slip in the shower. I'd been telling Mom and Dad we needed one, but they weren't listening. "Anything?"

"Anything."

"All right, I guess."

Sure enough, as soon as I walked around to Mrs. Harper's yard, she gave me a hug, a fourteen-year-long one. When she was finally done with all the hugging, she set me up at a table full of chipped plates and cups and a stuffed dead badger that she said was from when Mr. Harper was in his taxidermy phase. I knew it was a badger because its feet were glued to a piece of wood that said BADGER on it. She gave me a shoe box to put money in and gave me one last hug-squeeze and left. There wasn't anything I wanted at that table, but I thought I saw a stethoscope a couple tables over. It was either that or headphones. I'd have to check later.

It wasn't three seconds before stupid Doug Zimmerman from down the street spotted me and zoomed his way over to my table. He had a forest green bandanna wrapped around his forehead.

"Hello, Aaaaaannie," he said. He held the "An" part out really long, to be annoying I guess. "What are you doing?"

I straightened out the stuff on the table—a waffle iron, an old pair of dolphin socks, a suitcase with a typewriter inside it—and didn't even look at him. "I'm helping Mrs. Harper. What's it look like?"

He shrugged and picked up the waffle iron. "You going to the Fourth of July picnic this year?" he asked, opening up the waffle iron and closing it again. "We could make an obstacle course."

"I don't like obstacle courses anymore," I said.

"Sure you do." He set down the waffle iron and opened up a box of playing cards. "We could make a real good one, half on the grass and half in the lake. And I could show you some good safari ninja tricks for keeping the geese away."

"You smell so bad, no geese'd go near you anyway," I said, grabbing the cards from him and setting them back on the table.

Doug stuck his tongue out, and I stuck mine out right back.

Ever since Doug's best friend Brad moved to Texas a month ago, he'd been trying to hang out with me, but no way that was going to work. Because no matter what Doug Zimmerman thought, we were not friends. We *might* have been friends in kindergarten, and *maybe* I used to go over to his house sometimes and help him build obstacle courses in his yard, with tires to leap through and chairs to crawl under and trees to climb up and everything. Which was sort of fun, I guess, if you liked that kind of thing. But then Brad showed up, and Doug stopped being my friend and started being a stupid annoying boy who called me "Annie Bananie" and pinched the underside of my arm in the lunch line. Which was why building an obstacle course with him wasn't exactly the number-one thing I felt like doing.

"Anyway," I told him, "obstacle courses are dangerous because you could fall and break your skull open. Are you gonna buy something or what? This yard sale is only for paying customers."

Doug just shrugged and picked up the badger. It was real heavy, so he had to hold it with both hands. "Is this thing real?" he asked, poking it in the left eyeball.

"Don't do that!" I yelled, and I grabbed it from him.

"You're going to ruin it and then no one will buy it."

"Maybe *I* want to buy it," he said.

"Do not."

"Do too. How much is it?"

I checked the price tag, which said $2.00. "Three dollars," I told him.

Doug stuck his hand in his pocket and pulled out a bunch of one-dollar bills, probably ten of them, so many that I wished I'd told him the stupid stuffed badger cost more. He handed me three and I grabbed them quick before he could change his mind.

"What are you going to do with it?" I asked him as I stuck the bills into the shoe box. I didn't like talking to him, but I was kind of wondering what you did with a stuffed dead badger once you bought one.

"I dunno." He tugged at the edge of his forehead bandanna. "Maybe I'll sneak it into Trent's room when he's sleeping and stick it right next to his bed. That'd give him the willies for sure. Might even pee his pants."

Doug and his brothers were always trying to scare

each other silly. Mostly they liked to hide in trees and leap out at each other when the other person wasn't expecting it, which Doug said was being a stealth safari ninja. But they did other stuff too, like once Aaron and Trent told Doug there were werewolves on the loose and then they snuck outside Doug's window while he was sleeping and howled all night long. You were supposed to scare the other person so bad he peed his pants, that was the rule. As far as I knew no one had peed them yet, but I didn't really want to ask.

"Don't you think that'd freak him out?" Doug asked me. He sounded real excited about it.

I rolled my eyes and went back to straightening stuff on the table. I was hoping that if I pretended Doug wasn't there, he'd go away. But I guess that didn't work, because he kept talking.

"Hey, you want to know something?"

"Nope." I stacked a ballerina plate on top of a tap dancer one.

"Yes you do. It's interesting."

"Nuh-uh."

"How do you know? You haven't even heard what it is yet."

"So tell me already then."

"Okay, I will." Doug took a deep breath like he was going to say the most important thing there was. "Someone bought the old haunted house across the street."

"No they didn't."

"Did so."

The house across the street from ours had been empty for a while, ever since the Krazinskys moved out a year before. Rebecca was the one who decided it was haunted. She said the reason no one wanted to move in was because it was cursed, and she made me go over there a million times, trying to peek in the windows. Rebecca was wild for spooky stories, and she was dying to find out what the inside of a real haunted house looked like. Only too bad for us all the windows had blinds on them, so we never even saw the edge of a haunted carpet, no matter how hard we tried.

I wouldn't ever say it to Rebecca, but I was pretty

sure the house wasn't haunted. For one thing, it didn't *look* haunted. It wasn't old and spooky-looking, and not a single one of the windows was even boarded up. Rebecca said that a house didn't have to be spooky to be haunted, maybe that was the ghosts' secret trick to lure people in with their un-boarded-up windows, but I didn't believe that. Because for another thing, I didn't think there were really any ghosts. I didn't know what happened when you died, if there was heaven like Mrs. Harper said, or if it was more like what Mr. L. told me one time, where it was just the end, no sadness, no happiness or anything. But I was pretty sure that after Jared died, he didn't do stupid stuff like hang out in the Krazinskys' house howling at dust bunnies. I figured he was smarter than that. But Rebecca believed it for certain, and anyway it was fun trying to peek through the windows.

I kept on with the plate stacking, but I guess Doug wasn't through talking about the haunted house. "Someone bought it," he said. "They're moving in tomorrow."

"I don't believe you," I said.

"Well, it's true. Mr. L. told me. Hey! This badger is only two dollars. You said three."

"That's 'cause Mrs. Harper told me the price tag was a mistake. It's really three."

"Liar. Give me my dollar back." He reached for the shoe box with the money in it, but I squeezed it close to my chest.

"Can't give it back," I said. "There's a lot of dollars in here and I don't remember which one's yours anymore."

He growled at me for a while, but I wouldn't give him that dollar. Thank goodness Mr. Harper finally came over and said he had a collection of shark teeth Doug might be interested in, because I'd heard one time that being around someone you hated could give you allergic reactions, and I was pretty sure Doug was starting to give me hives.

three
●●●

I stayed at that table the whole rest of the morning, organizing all the stuff so it looked nice and pretty. Mrs. Harper even brought me two cups of lemonade. It wasn't too bad a job, really, because I got to be in charge of stuff and talk to people. I kept glancing at the not-really-haunted house across the street, wondering who was going to live there. When Rebecca got back from her ballet class later, I could go over and tell her about it. She'd want our new neighbors to be zombies or vampires, I bet. Something spooky. I just hoped they didn't have a mean dog, like a pit bull or something, because I'd seen on the news one time how pit bulls could attack you when you least expected it.

Round about eleven I started to notice the sun huge in the sky like a yellow beach ball, and I realized I wasn't wearing any sunscreen. Which was bad, because you could get a sunburn even in the shade, and sunburns gave you skin cancer, and that could kill you. I learned that from a brochure at the doctor's office.

I tucked the shoe box tight up under my armpit and found Mrs. Harper, who was selling pillowcases to a lady I didn't know. I tried not to be fidgety while Mrs. Harper counted out change, but I swear I could feel the rays from the sun warming up my skin and making cancer molecules right there. I yanked on Mrs. Harper's elbow.

She ignored me. "Here's two dollars back," she told the lady.

I yanked again. "Mrs. Harper?"

When the lady with the pillowcases finally left, Mrs. Harper said, "Yes, dear? How's it going?"

"Good," I said. "I mean, okay. I mean, I might be getting cancer."

"Sorry?" She tilted her head to the side.

"Here." I held out the shoe box for her. "I have to go home before I get sunburned."

"Oh," she said, and she laughed tinkly like a bell. "Well, you know, I have some sunscreen if you'd like to use it. Then you can stay for a while. Only if you want to, of course."

I thought about that. I wouldn't mind helping some more, as long as it didn't give me cancer. "What SPF is it?" I asked. Ours at home was only fifteen, which according to the brochure was not very high, but Mom said she wasn't buying more until we used it up.

"Forty, I think," Mrs. Harper said.

"You have anything else?" I asked. "Like SPF a thousand?"

"I don't think it goes that high, dear."

"Oh."

"It's in the cabinet in the bathroom," she told me. And then she turned to help a woman holding a purple turtleneck sweater.

I went into the house and I found the sunscreen in

the bathroom, right where Mrs. Harper said it would be. I spread it everywhere I had skin showing, my arms and legs and even my earlobes. I was extra careful to get every centimeter of my face, because the skin on your face is supersensitive, that's what the brochure said. But I made sure not to get any in my eyes.

When I was walking back outside, I passed the bookshelf in the hallway. Mr. and Mrs. Harper had a million trillion books, all stacked on top of each other and spilling off the bookshelves, and I'd never really looked at any of them before. But just at that moment, I noticed a big green fat one, with a spine as big as my fist, that was poked out just a couple inches farther than the other ones. Trailing down the spine in thick yellow letters were the words: *The Everyday Guide to Preventing Illness.*

I yanked it off the shelf.

I flipped through it and knew right away it was exactly what I needed. The book had everything— smallpox and liver disease and acid reflux and anemia, and what to do to once you got it and how to make sure you never got it in the first place. It was perfect, just perfect.

I found Mrs. Harper outside lining up baby shoes in a tidy straight row.

"Mrs. Harper?"

"Yes, dear?" she said, looking up from the shoes. "What've you got there?"

"A book. I found it in the hallway."

She took it from me. "Ah, yes," she said, after she'd read the title. "It's one of Mr. Harper's. From his physician phase."

"Can I have it for my freebie?"

"Your freebie?"

"Yeah. You said if I helped out, I could pick one thing for free. Anything I wanted."

"Oh." She frowned. "I meant something out here. This book isn't for sale, honey."

"But—"

"Besides, I just can't make you work all this time and then send you home with an old medical book. Let's check out the toy table, shall we? I'm sure we'll find something nice over there." And she set the big green book down behind the baby shoes and stuck her fat hand behind my back, leading me over to the toys.

When we got to the toy table, Mrs. Harper showed me about one million things she thought I might like—LEGOs, an old dump truck, a doll with one eye permanently blinked closed—but there wasn't anything I wanted as much as that book. Mrs. Harper wouldn't give it to me, though.

Finally I picked a red wooden top, even though I hadn't played with tops since I was two. Mrs. Harper told me I'd made an excellent choice. I just nodded.

"Would you like to stick around for a little while longer, Annie?" she asked me. "You've been a great help."

I shook my head. "I think I'm going to see if Rebecca's back from ballet class. I want to tell her about the haunted house."

"The haunted house?"

"Yeah, you know, the one across the street. Someone's moving in tomorrow."

"Oh, yes," Mrs. Harper said. "I met her when she came to take a look at the house."

"Her?" I asked. "Is it a lady with a dog?"

She shook her head. "I'm afraid she doesn't have one, dear, sorry. Or any children, either, at least none your age. Mrs. Finch must be in her seventies at least."

"Oh," I said. "Well, I'm gonna go tell Rebecca then."

"Of course. Thanks so much for your help, Annie. I really appreciate it." She straightened up an old rag doll that was threatening to fall off the table. "And in case I don't see you before then, don't forget our Sunbird car wash on Tuesday. Nine A.M. sharp!"

"Yep. Thank you for the freebie," I said, because that was polite.

But what wasn't polite at all was what I did next, when I passed the table with the baby shoes on my way across the lawn—I picked that big green book right up and tucked it under my T-shirt, and hustled all the way back to my yard. I looked over my shoulder twice to see if Mrs. Harper noticed, but she was so busy sorting through her husband's harmonica collection that she never even looked my way.

The closer I got to my front door, the more I started to think that maybe I should turn around and put that book back. It was big and heavy and sweaty against my skin. If I ran back right that second, maybe I could slip it onto the baby shoe table without anyone noticing. I was pretty positive it wouldn't be stealing if I returned it before I really took it for good.

But then I looked up at my house and saw Jared's window, with his blue curtains shut up tight so you couldn't see inside, just the way it'd been since February.

There were lots of worse things to worry about than taking an old book, I realized. Because for all I knew, right that very second I could get bitten by a rattlesnake and need to know how to suck out the poison, or I could step on a nail and get tetanus, or I could develop a cough that turned out to be bronchitis. And there were probably millions of more things I didn't even know about, and the only way to make sure

I was always safe and that nothing bad could happen to me was to know exactly what could get me and all the ways to stop it. I had to be prepared, that was all there was to it.

I took one last look at the Harpers' yard over the hedge, at the empty spot on the table where the big green book had been. And then, before I had a chance to change my mind, I turned the doorknob to my house and ran up the stairs two at a time to my room. If I was going to read that entire book before anything got me, I figured I better get started right away.

four
●●●

I read the big green book for almost two hours, lying on my back on the floor with my feet up on my bed. There was some real good stuff in there, all about scarlet fever and lactose intolerance, and how you should check your carbon monoxide detectors every week to make sure they were working. I stuck slips of paper between the pages to mark all the important stuff, which was pretty much everything. But some of the words were too long and confusing for me, and anyway after a while my eyeballs started to get fuzzy. When I looked that up, it turned out it was a sign of diabetes. I figured I should stop reading so they wouldn't get any fuzzier.

I decided to go over to Rebecca's to tell her about the haunted house, like I'd told Mrs. Harper I would. And maybe while I was there, Rebecca's dad would let me borrow a dictionary so I could understand the book better. We used to have a dictionary at our house, a nice good fat one, but Jared had lost it about a year ago when he'd taken it to school for a language arts project and left it on the bus afterward.

Rebecca lived only twelve houses away from me, on the other side of the street. If you squinted real hard from my living-room window, you could see Rebecca's mom when she was watering the lawn. As soon as I got there, I took off all my gear and stacked it next to my bike in the far corner of Rebecca's driveway, where it wouldn't be in the way of cars and cause an accident, and then I rang the doorbell. Rebecca's dad answered.

"Hi there, Annie!" he said. Dr. Young always sounded happy to see me. "How are you feeling today?"

"I'm okay," I said. "Except I think I might have African sleeping sickness."

His eyebrows squinched close together when I said that, bunched up in the middle confused. "It's unlikely," he told me. He put his hand on my forehead. "But I can take your temperature if it'd make you feel better."

"Thanks."

I walked through the house to the kitchen and sat myself on a stool at the counter.

"Here we go," Dr. Young told me, once he'd fished the thermometer out of the drawer. He gave it to me, and I wedged it solid under my tongue.

You weren't supposed to chitchat while you were waiting for a thermometer to beep, so while Dr. Young started up a pot of coffee, I checked the word wall to see if there was anything new.

Even though Rebecca's dad was a doctor, I always thought he should have been a book writer instead, because he was just crazy for words. He had stacks and stacks of books all over the house, even in the bathroom. And when he found a word he liked—one he said struck his fancy because it sounded silly or had a peculiar meaning—he'd grab a piece of chalk and write the word in big doctor-squiggly letters on the giant chalkboard on the far wall in the kitchen. Sometimes if he couldn't find any chalk, he'd rip the page right out of his book and circle the words he liked, and then tape it up there. The whole chalkboard was covered in words, every sort of one you could think of—*homily, emaciate, herbivore, tonsillectomy, waterfall, egg drop soup, wisp, Francophile, jurisdiction.* I had no idea what most of the words meant, and neither did Rebecca, but we liked to stare at the wall and try to figure it out. Dr. Young was always saying how we should play with words, so I never was sure why it made him laugh so hard the time he found us acting out "Goldilocks and the Three Proboscises."

My thermometer beeped just as the coffee started hissing into the pot. Dr. Young showed me the temperature. "Ninety-eight point six," he said. "Perfect."

"So I don't have African sleeping sickness?"

"Nope." He shook the thermometer. "Where did

you hear about a thing like that, anyway?"

"From a book," I said. Which reminded me of the thing I wanted to ask him. "Hey, Dr. Young? Do you have a dictionary I could borrow? This new book I'm reading has millions of long words in it I don't know, so I want to look them up."

"Good for you, Annie," he said, and he smiled big. "Which one would you like? *Webster's, Oxford English, Brewer's Dictionary of Phrase and Fable*? I have dozens."

I thought about that. "Just a real fat one, I think. The fattest one you have."

"I know exactly the one then," he said. "Actually, it's right"—he reached up above his head and opened a cupboard, where there were tons of cookbooks and phone books and pieces of paper mashed all together— "here. There you go. You think you can carry that home without any mishaps?"

It really was big, the hugest dictionary I'd ever seen, and it must've weighed more than three watermelons. "Yep," I said. "My bike has a basket. Thanks."

"Sure thing. So what's this book you're reading?"

"*The Everyday Guide to Preventing Illness*," I told him. "It has lots of good stuff in there. So I don't get sick and die."

I thought Dr. Young would be proud of me for trying to be a good disease catcher, like he was. But when I looked up at him, he was frowning into his mug of coffee while he stirred it slowly with a spoon. "Annie," he said after a while, "do you know what *despondent* means?"

I shook my head.

"Well, then." He rummaged around in a drawer until he found a piece of chalk, and then he wrote the word *despondent* on the word wall in big squiggly letters. Chalk dust fell to the ground as he crossed the *t*. He didn't tell me what it meant. I think he wanted me to look it up in the dictionary. But I could tell by the dead-brother look he was giving me as he set the chalk on the counter that I didn't want to.

"Why don't we go find Rebecca?" he said after a little bit. "I think she's in the backyard with her mom."

I didn't answer at first, just studied the black-and-white tiles on the kitchen floor. One of them was chipped, which I'd never noticed before. "Dr. Young?" I said.

"Yes?" He picked up his coffee mug, his chalky fingers leaving marks on the handle.

"If you'd been at the hospital that day, instead of that other doctor, I mean . . ." I smoothed my hands over my legs. My palms were sweatier than normal. I was going to have to check that one in the big green book when I got home to see if it was a symptom of any bad diseases. "Do you think you would've figured out about Jared's heart?" I asked. "Do you think you could've fixed him?"

"Oh, Annie," Dr. Young said, and he set his mug back on the counter even though he hadn't taken any sips. "I must have asked myself that very same question at least a hundred times."

But he didn't tell me the answer, just stood there scratching his cheek.

"Yeah?" I said.

He took a deep breath, like he needed lots of air

to help push out the words he was going to say. "I know the doctor who saw your brother that day. Dr. Amundsen. She's a good friend of mine, actually, and an excellent doctor. Annie, what your brother had, an aortic dissection, it's extremely uncommon, especially in someone his age. And if Dr. Amundsen didn't figure it out, I don't know that anyone could have."

"Oh," I said. I wasn't sure if that made me feel better or worse. "But—"

"The most important thing, however," Dr. Young said, "is that *you* are healthy." He picked up his coffee again and took a long sip, but his eyes were on me the whole time. "You know that, right, Annie?" he said after he was done swallowing his coffee sip. "You're not going to get what Jared had. You're perfectly healthy, inside and out."

I squeezed the dictionary closer to my chest. "Mmm," I said.

Dr. Young looked like he was going to say something else then, but before he got a chance, Rebecca came into the kitchen.

"Hi, Annie!" she said when she saw me. Her two blond braids were falling down her back, same as always, and she was carrying her hamster's cage, with all its neon pink and yellow crawling tubes sticking out everywhere. "I didn't even know you were here."

"Yep." I pointed to the hamster cage in her arms. "What are you doing with Fuzzby?"

"Mom said I have to clean his cage because he's looking *peaked*."

"Ooh!" Dr. Young said. "*Peaked*! Fabulous word." And he scribbled it on the wall.

I peered inside Fuzzby's cage. "He's sleeping," I said. Fuzzby was always sleeping. He hardly ever did anything except every once in a while he'd *squeak-squeak-squeak* in his hamster wheel, and that was only when me and Rebecca were having sleepovers and were finally at the sleeping part.

"Yeah," Rebecca said. "Except normally he sleeps up top and now he's right next to his food dish."

"Maybe he has seasonal affective disorder," I told her. I'd read about that one that morning. "You can get it in the winter and it makes you real tired and sad."

Rebecca frowned. "But it's the summer," she said. "And he's a hamster."

"Let me take a look," Dr. Young said. He opened up the top part of the cage and scooped Fuzzby out with one hand. Fuzzby blinked his eyes open sleepy sleepy. He didn't look too happy about being woken up.

While Dr. Young examined Fuzzby, Rebecca took apart all the parts of the hamster cage and dumped out the wood chips at the bottom and then filled the sink with soapy water to dunk the hamster tubes in. I hated when Rebecca had to clean Fuzzby's cage, because it took forever and it smelled disgusting, sick-sweet like fruit punch that spilled in the carpet a million years ago. But I decided I should be a good friend and help anyway. So I dug out the yellow rubber gloves from under the sink and gave one pair to Rebecca and put one pair on my own hands, and we got to cleaning.

"Well?" Rebecca asked her dad while she scrubbed a tiny hamster poop off the squeak wheel. "Is he okay?"

"I think he's fine," Dr. Young said. "But I'm no

hamster expert. His breathing might be a little more shallow than normal. If he's still looking lethargic tomorrow, we'll take him to the vet, okay?"

"Okay," Rebecca said.

Dr. Young put Fuzzby in a giant mixing bowl on the counter and picked up his mug again. "I'm going to go find your mother," he said to Rebecca. "Annie, good luck with that book of yours."

I looked up from my suds. "Thanks," I said.

I thought he was going to leave the kitchen right then, but he didn't. Instead he took a sip of his coffee, nodded his head at me, and said, "Not all words are helpful, you know." Which I thought was pretty weird.

"So guess what," I told Rebecca once Dr. Young had left the kitchen with his coffee.

"What?"

"Someone's moving into the haunted house."

"Really?" As soon as I said "haunted house," Rebecca's eyes got big as Ping-Pong balls. "Is it a ghost?"

"Nah. It's just an old lady. She doesn't have a pit

43

bull." I rinsed off the last neon pink tube. "I think she's moving in tomorrow."

"Man!" Rebecca said, taking her gloves off to start on the drying part. "How are we ever going to sneak into the yard to see inside if someone *lives* there?"

Rebecca started thinking. I could tell that was what she was doing, because whenever Rebecca thought real hard, she chewed on the end of one of her braids. Her mom always braided her hair in two long pieces, every single day. Rebecca had real pretty hair, twice as long as mine and the exact same color as the split in the top of her mom's loaf of fresh-baked bread. I know because we checked it. We tried to figure out what color my hair was once and it turned out it was the same as the dirt at the very bottom of Mr. L.'s compost pile. Which in my opinion was not nearly as nice a color as bread.

Rebecca pulled her braid out of her mouth and said, "We've got to find a way to get in there and see the ghosts."

"I guess."

"But now if we break in, we'll get caught for sure,

with that old lady and everything."

I rubbed the bottom part of Fuzzby's cage with a dish towel. I didn't care so much about getting inside the haunted house, but I could tell Rebecca thought it'd be better than Disneyland in there. "Well, what if we didn't break in?" I said. "What if we just"—an idea was starting to tingle at the sides of my brain—"visited?"

Rebecca chewed some more, and then said, "But what would we visit her for? She's an old lady."

"Well, maybe we could bring her something. Like a present. And then when she was opening it, we'd sneak inside and find all the ghosts."

"Yeah," Rebecca said, and she was grinning now. "Yeah. And you know what we could bring her? A casserole."

"A casserole?"

"That's what Mrs. Harper brought us when we moved here."

"But I don't know how to make casserole."

"Me neither." Rebecca frowned.

I tried to think some more while we dried, and

Rebecca chewed faster than ever. But by the time we'd finished with Fuzzby's cage, and all the tubes were clicked back into place, and we'd put a fresh layer of wood chips at the bottom and new food in the food bowl and water in the water bottle, we still hadn't thought of anything. Rebecca stuck Fuzzby back inside and shrugged her shoulders at me.

"You wanna ride bikes?" she asked. "We could do turtle tracks if you want. Maybe that'll give us some good ideas."

"Sure," I said. Turtle tracks was the game I made up three months ago, where you rode your bike as slow as possible without coming to a stop. It was the opposite of racing. Whoever took the longest to get to the finish line was the winner. So far the record was five minutes to get from Mrs. Harper's petunia bed to my mailbox. We used to ride races all the time, and I could tell Rebecca liked that more, but I didn't think racing was such a good idea. Because even with a helmet on, if you got going too fast, you could crash into a tree and get paralyzed. I read about it in the newspaper.

"Great!" Rebecca said. "Let me just get my helmet." She leaned over in front of Fuzzby's cage so she was eye to eye with him and said, "Don't worry, Fuzz. You'll be just fine." And then she picked up the cage and headed to her room.

When Rebecca got back, I was staring at the word wall, that word *despondent* staring back at me. I didn't like it.

"I'm ready to go!" Rebecca hollered at me, her bike helmet already strapped to her head. For some reason she always talked super loud whenever she was wearing her bike helmet, even if I was standing right next to her.

I lugged the dictionary off the counter and looked back at the word wall, trying to find the perfect shouting-out word. And then I found it.

"Shish-kebab!" I said.

"Shish-kebab!" Rebecca cried back. And we raced for the door.

five

●●●

When I woke up Sunday morning, there was a word rolling around in my brain, the word *despondent,* and for a second I couldn't figure out where it came from. But then I remembered it was the dead-brother word Dr. Young had written up on his word wall. I wriggled out of bed and found the dictionary and plunked it open on the floor. You could tell just by looking inside that it was a Dr. Young dictionary, because there were squiggly notes all up and down the margins, and half the pages were marked with Post-its or tiny pieces of paper, and some words were highlighted and other ones were circled or had check marks next to them. It was like a word jungle in there, and you had to trek through all the scribbles to find the word you wanted.

Des Moines, desperado, despise . . . Yep, there it was, *despondent.* "In low spirits from loss of hope or courage." That's what it said.

I thumped the dictionary closed.

Dr. Young was the one who'd told me I was perfectly healthy, inside and out, and now he was saying I was *despondent*? Well, he was wrong about that one too. I wasn't despondent, I knew that. I was . . . I opened the dictionary up again just to make sure I had the right word, and finally I found it, outlined with a rectangle in dark blue ink. *Cautious.* "Attentive to potential problems or dangers."

I read the big green book for a while, learning about lots more diseases and sicknesses and stuff. When I went downstairs for breakfast, Dad was in the kitchen already, sitting at the table reading the paper.

"Good morning, Moonbeam," he said, shaking the

fold part in the paper just a teeny bit so it stuck up straight. He took a sip of coffee, still reading.

"Hi," I said. Then I stood there in the doorway, frozen still like a Popsicle, to see if maybe he'd remember.

It used to be, on Sundays, Dad and I would read the newspaper together, him sipping his coffee and me snuggled in close in the chair right next to him. We'd read the whole thing, front to back, even the stuff I didn't always understand, like what the president said about China, and floods and stock markets and everything. We'd been doing it for as long as I could remember, since before I could read a single word myself. Every Sunday I'd come down to the kitchen early, still in my pajamas, and Dad would be there, already sipping his coffee. And he'd smile at me and say, "Good morning, Moonbeam. Care to read with me?" And I'd squeeze right up next to him with my cereal bowl, and we'd spend the whole morning reading. Sometimes I even helped him with the crossword, because he said I was his good luck charm for finishing.

But we hadn't done that since February, not once

since Jared died. Every Sunday I'd wait and wait, but Dad only ever remembered the "Good morning, Moonbeam" part, and forgot the rest.

Dad turned a page in the paper. "Got any fun plans today?" he asked, shaking the newspaper flat again.

I just shrugged. "I might go to Rebecca's when she's back from church."

"Oh," he said, eyeballs stuck like glue to his newspaper. "Well, that sounds fun."

"Yeah."

Maybe he didn't forget the second part, I thought. Maybe he just didn't feel like reading with me anymore.

After I found the cereal I wanted in the cupboard, I opened up the bread box on the counter just to make sure my bread was in there. I'd saved half an old loaf of sandwich bread, and I'd told Mom and Dad about fifty times not to throw it away, but you never could be sure about things like that. I'd put it in there a week ago, and I was waiting for it to get good and stale, so we could feed it to the ducks on Tuesday, when we went to the Fourth of July picnic at the lake. We did that every year, feeding the ducks. You got five points if more than one duck went for your piece, and ten if one of them caught it in its mouth. Jared made that part up. I poked the bread through the bag. Good and stale, just the way the ducks liked it.

Mom came into the kitchen and gave me a kiss on the forehead. "Hello, sweetie," she said. Then she saw the box I was holding. "Annie Richards," she said with a smile squished up in the corner of her mouth, "are you eating your father's *bran flakes* for breakfast?" I nodded and she laughed, plopping a slice of nonstale bread into the toaster. "No Loco Cocoas today? I thought those were your favorite."

"Nah," I said, getting out a bowl from the cupboard. "Anyway, it's Cocoa Locos. And I'm watching my fiber. So I can prevent against colon cancer." I poured in the milk.

Mom sighed. "You realize that you absolutely do not need to be worrying about colon cancer at your age, don't you? What even put that in your head?"

"This new book I got," I said, putting the milk back in the fridge. "It's a real good one. It tells you all the things to watch out for."

Mom turned to look at Dad like he might have something to say about that, but he was busy reading the newspaper, not even listening at all. "Annie," she said again in her Mom voice, all concern and wrinkles, "you know I don't like you worrying so much. You are absolutely fine. Reading that book is only going to make you *think* you're sick."

"But what if I really am, and just no one knows it yet?" I said. "You thought Jared was fine too, until—"

"Annie!" she said, and she sounded real mad. But then her face went back to normal so fast, I thought maybe I made the madness up. "Just eat your breakfast, all right?"

So I sat down at the table across from Dad, with my cereal and a spoon. I thought about asking if we could get soy milk at the grocery store later, because the book had said that was healthier than regular, but then I saw Mom scrubbing at the stovetop with a sponge and I figured it was best not to ask her. When her bread popped up out of the toaster, she didn't even bother to get it.

After one bite of my cereal, I realized that bran flakes might be good for you, but they tasted worse than dog food. When I grew up, I was going to figure out a way to make Cocoa Locos the healthiest food on Earth. I mashed my cereal down the garbage disposal and grabbed a banana from the fruit bowl. Then I found my pencil with the star-shaped eraser and my old science notebook in the den, and I went outside to sit on the porch steps, careful to sit down in a spot that didn't look too splintery.

If there was one thing that big green book had made me realize, it was that I couldn't wait any longer to make a will. Cholesterol, typhoid fever, ticks, rabies, lung cancer. There was tons of stuff that could get me, and I wasn't even halfway through the book yet. Plus there were loads of things that weren't even in there—nondisease things, like crashing airplanes and runaway zoo animals and earthquakes and falling off the monkey bars. And hockey pucks. You never knew what was going to get you, and you never knew when. Jared's twelfth birthday was exactly one week away, and he hadn't made it to that. So who knew how long I'd be around?

I opened up my science notebook to a blank page in the back and propped it up against my knee. Then I peeled my banana and chewed it slow, one bite at a time, staring at the blue lines in my notebook and thinking about what I was going to put down there. And when I was all done eating, I had it. I licked the tip of my pencil, the way they did sometimes in movies, and I began to write.

Annie Richards's Will

That's what I wrote at the top. I did it in my very best handwriting, so the *A* in my name came to a perfect point and each *s* was two even curves. It was so pretty that if Miss Kimball had seen it, she would've felt awful about giving me a U for Unsatisfactory in penmanship.

Then came the harder part. I sat there for what felt like an hour, kicking my heel against the bottom step and thinking about what it was I wanted to leave people—Chirpy and my snow globe and my roller skates and all my board games. Finally I did have a list, and I thought it was okay.

I, Annie Richards, hereby leave the following stuff to people, just in case I die from yellow fever or something else bad.

All my toys and clothes and things like that go to Rebecca Young, and also she can have my glitter pens that she's had her eye on ever since I got them. And my stuffed turtle, Chirpy, too, but only if she lets him sit on her bed all the time, right by the pillows.

Tommy Lippowitz gets all the books on my bookshelf because he likes to read, except the horse ones he doesn't want he can just leave there I guess.

My pictures I took at the beach last year and my blue ribbon from the Math Olympics are for my mom and dad.

Mrs. Harper can have all my Junior Sunbird stuff, so maybe someone else can use it if they join Junior Sunbirds and they're my same size so then they don't have to buy a new ugly outfit for themselves and can just have mine.

Doug Zimmerman doesn't get anything.

There were other things I wasn't sure what to do with—like my diary, for one. Because I didn't think I wanted anyone to know my secret business, like that I thought our principal, Mr. Oliver, was the handsomest man on the planet. But after a while I decided if I felt a real bad sickness coming on, I could throw the diary in the garbage so no one could read it. And all the other stuff probably wasn't important anyway.

At the end I wrote

This is my very official will, the end.
Signed, Anne Emily Richards

When I was done, I ripped the page out of my notebook and folded it up into a square. And just so everyone would know that it was an extra-important document, and that no matter what they had to do what it said, I wrote a word on the outside in thick capital printing, each letter as big as a lima bean. It was a word from Dr. Young's word wall.

INDESTRUCTIBLE.

And I underlined it three times. Then for safekeeping I stuck the folded-up will in my back shorts pocket, the one that was pink-and-blue and shaped like a flower.

I was just thinking about going inside to get some Cocoa Locos, because I didn't think they could be *too* unhealthy, otherwise the cereal company wouldn't be able to make them, and anyway I was pretty much starving. But right then a moving truck pulled into the driveway of the haunted house across the street, and that made my stomach stop grumbling. Two muscly men hopped out of the truck and slid the back door up. I leaned forward to watch as they unloaded things. I wanted to see if there'd be anything haunted-looking I could tell Rebecca about when she got back from church.

Pretty much, though, it looked like normal stuff. There was furniture and rugs and lots and lots of cardboard boxes. The only thing that was weird at all was that one of the boxes had FRAGILE! written on the side in red letters so big you could probably see them from the top of Mount Everest. But I didn't think Rebecca would be too interested in that. Maybe I'd tell her I saw a swarm of black cats or something.

After a while a car parked on the street out front, and out stepped a lady who must've been Mrs. Finch. She was boring as socks in a drawer, with short white hair that was cut close to her head in an old-lady haircut, and maroon slacks with creases so straight you could've used them for rulers. She reminded me of the friendly old ladies who always stopped outside Lippy's when we were selling Junior Sunbird cookies, the ones you could tell didn't even like sweets but always bought six boxes of Royal Chocolate Ripples anyway.

That was it!

I jumped to the balls of my feet and my science notebook clattered down the steps, but I didn't care. I'd figured out exactly how we were going to get inside the haunted house.

six
● ● ●

"Annie?" my mom called from out in the hallway.

"In here, Mom!"

I was lying on my stomach on my bed, with the big green book open on my right to the section called "Cholera and Other Waterborne Diseases," and the Dr. Young dictionary open on my left to the page with the word *waterborne* on it.

Mom stepped into the room. "Annie, Rebecca's here."

"Really?" I snapped my head up. I'd been waiting

for over an hour for Rebecca's family to get back from church so I could tell her my genius idea about getting into the haunted house.

"She's downstairs," Mom said. Then she peered down at my book. "What are you reading, *Moby-Dick*?"

"Nah," I said. "It's that book I was telling you about." I rolled over on my back, which made me accidentally squash the dictionary. "All about diseases and stuff. It's really helpful. Also I've figured out that I probably don't have leukemia."

Mom closed her eyes for a second and took in a big deep breath, slow and noisy. When she opened up her eyes again, she reached over me and plonked the big green book closed.

"Mom!" I cried. "I didn't even put a bookmark in there."

She picked the book up with two hands. "Annie, I really don't think this is a good book for you to be reading."

"But—"

"You do not have leukemia. You do not have cholera. You are just *fine*. Do you understand me?"

"But—"

"Now why don't you go downstairs and say hi to Rebecca?"

I sat up on my bed. "Can I have my book back at least?"

"We'll talk about it later."

"But—"

"*Annie.*"

"Fine."

I trudged out of the room while Mom waited in the doorway, still holding on to my book. I tried to lurk around at the top of the stairs for a while to see what she was going to do with it, but she saw me peeking and gave me a *look*, so I had to give up.

When I got to the front door, Rebecca was waiting for me, her bike helmet strapped to her head. "Hi, Annie!" she hollered at me because of the helmet. "I got your signal!"

"Which one?" I said. I was still wondering what

Mom had done with my book. I hoped she was going to give it back. I hadn't gotten to read anything about jaundice or ringworm or high blood pressure yet, and those sounded like important ones.

"The leaf!" Rebecca shouted.

"Oh, good." I'd stuck a leaf halfway under Rebecca's front door. That was our secret signal we used, to let the other person know that we had something important to talk about. But just in case the leaf blew away, we had a backup secret signal, which was leaving a message on the answering machine.

"So! What did you want to tell me!"

I smiled then, because I knew Rebecca was going to like my idea. "It's about—" I pointed over Rebecca's shoulder at the haunted house. "And how to get inside." Her eyes got Ping-Pong ball huge again.

We went upstairs to my room, because that's where our secret planning spot was, in the space between my desk and the wall. The dictionary was still lying out open on the bed, but the big green book was gone, and so was Mom. I sighed.

"What!" Rebecca shouted.

I tapped my head, so she'd know to take off her bike helmet, and she did. "What is it?" she asked again, quieter. "What's wrong?"

"Nothing," I said.

"Oh good," she said, and she tucked herself into the planning spot. "So tell me how we can get into the haunted house."

I squeezed in right next to her, up against the desk. "Okay. We're gonna sell Mrs. Finch some cookies."

"Cookies?"

I nodded. "Junior Sunbird ones." And I told her my whole plan, all about how I would pretend to be selling cookies, and Rebecca would hide behind Mrs. Finch's tree, and when Mrs. Finch went to get her checkbook, Rebecca would race quick like a fox into the house and look around while I did some distracting.

Rebecca stuck a braid in her mouth and started chewing. I didn't say anything, just let her think, and after a minute or two she spit her braid out. You could tell the part she'd sucked on because it was darker than the rest of her hair. "That's a really good plan," she told me.

"Really?"

"Definitely."

The one bad part of my idea was that I had to wear my Junior Sunbird outfit, and I hated that thing more than black licorice jelly beans. One time Jared said it made me look like a blob of chewed-up purple bubble gum, and he was right. Plus there were only three badges on my sash, and one was what they gave you for showing up on the first day. Rebecca had twelve, and she'd been in the troop the same amount of time as me, only obviously she was lots better at sewing and hiking and stuff. So my Junior Sunbird outfit wasn't exactly my favorite thing. But Rebecca said it wouldn't look real if I didn't wear it, and if it didn't look real, Rebecca wouldn't be able to sneak inside the house. So I put it on.

We walked across the street together, me dressed up ugly and purple, and Rebecca with my dad's bird-watching binoculars hanging around her neck. She probably could've seen fine without them, but Rebecca really liked my dad's bird-watching binoculars. Just as we reached the corner of Mrs. Finch's yard, where the big oak tree was, Rebecca grabbed my arm and I stopped walking.

"Are you sure you're going to be okay?" she asked me.

"I think so," I said, but all of a sudden that got me worrying. "Why? You think something bad's going to happen?" What if Mrs. Finch had laryngitis and she coughed on me? What if I dislocated my kneecap going up the stairs? How was I supposed to fix any of that myself if Mom had taken my book away?

Rebecca chewed on her hair. "Well," she said after thinking awhile, "I guess you'll be fine. I mean, if any ghosts start flying out when the door opens, you can just duck and they probably won't get you."

I was pretty sure I rolled my eyes at that one, but Rebecca didn't notice. "Okay," I said. I started for the door, hanging on tight to a box of Coconut Babies with my left hand and crossing my fingers with the right one.

I was almost to the door when from behind me Rebecca called out, "Annie?" I turned. Rebecca was already hidden behind the tree, with only her head poking out to talk to me. "If you get in trouble," she said, "just whistle." And she gave me her best Sunbird salute.

I nodded, even though I didn't know how to whistle.

Before I even climbed up the last step of the porch, Mrs. Finch opened up her door to greet me. "Why, hello there!" she said, all smiles. I took a good look at her. She didn't look like she had any bad diseases, although you could never know for sure. But she looked mostly like a regular old lady, plain as a box of toothpicks, except for her short white hair that came to pointed curls like the tops of the lemon meringue pie Rebecca's mom sometimes made.

"Oh, dear," she said to me, before I even had a chance to say anything myself. "Did you hurt yourself?"

"Huh?"

"Your arms," she said.

"Oh." I looked down at my Band-Aids. "I'm okay," I told her. "None of them are deadly."

"Well, that's good to hear." Mrs. Finch straightened up her back and smiled. "Can I help you with something?"

I shook my head side to side. "Nope," I said. "No, thank you."

"Really? I thought maybe you were selling cookies."

"Oh yeah," I said, remembering. "Yeah, I'm selling cookies." I gave her the Sunbird salute.

Her eyes seemed lit up a little bit, and I couldn't tell if she was laughing at me or if she was just an eye-lighting-up kind of person.

"What kinds do you have?" she asked.

"Just this box of Coconut Babies." I held it out for her to inspect. "It's the last one left." I was hoping Mrs. Finch wouldn't look at it too close before she went for her checkbook, because one of the corners was seriously dented. Rebecca and I had found it in the very back of my kitchen cupboard, and I had a feeling that it might be older than the president. Which wasn't too surprising, really, because Coconut Babies tasted like the inside of a shoe and no one ever wanted to eat them.

"Well, coconut isn't my favorite," Mrs. Finch said. "But I do like to support the Sunbirds." She held her hand out for the box then, so I gave it to her.

"It's five dollars," I said.

All of a sudden Mrs. Finch made a noise that sounded a lot like a snort. She looked up from the cookie box with a smile on her face that reminded me of a hot water bottle, warm from the inside. She held up the Coconut Babies and pointed to a date on the side. "Have you been selling all your customers expired goods, dear?"

"Um . . . ," I said. The cookie plan was obviously not working. My mind gears started up, trying to think of another way to distract Mrs. Finch so Rebecca could get inside her house. "Can I use your bathroom?" I said at last, leaning over to see past Mrs. Finch.

She laughed. "Spying on the new neighbor, are we?"

"What? No." I stood up straight. "I just have to pee."

"Ah. So why does your friend need the binoculars?"

I whirled around. Rebecca had half her whole body poked out from behind the tree, my dad's binoculars held up to her face.

"What is it?" Rebecca shouted at me. "What's going on?"

"*Whistle!*" I hollered back at her. "Whistle! Whistle! Whistle!" And I bolted down the steps and down the lawn, all the way across the street, Rebecca right beside me. I lost the box of Coconut Babies somewhere near the oak tree.

Once we were back safe inside my house with the door slammed shut tight, Rebecca and I hid beneath the living-room window and took turns looking at Mrs. Finch's house through my dad's binoculars. Mrs. Finch was still standing on her porch, chuckling.

"She thinks we're crazy," Rebecca said, handing me the binoculars for good and scooching down underneath the window, her back to the wall. "No way we're going to get inside there now."

"Yeah," I said, and I knew she was right. I peered through the binoculars again at my new nonspooky neighbor. "At least she doesn't have laryngitis, though."

Rebecca folded her arms across her chest. "Ghosts don't have laryngitis either," she said. And I had to admit she was right about that one.

seven

●●●

Rebecca stayed at my house the rest of the afternoon, the two of us trying to think up new plans to get into the haunted house, but we couldn't come up with anything.

"What if we just keep looking in the windows?" I said for the four hundredth time. "Sooner or later she's going to forget to shut the blinds, and then we'll be able to see inside."

Rebecca shook her head so hard, her braids smacked into the sides of her face. "No way," she said. "You had a really great idea, about going inside. I don't want to just *look.* I want to be *in* there." She gnawed on her braid for a while, and then I guess she must've thought of something good, because all at once she spit the braid right out. "How about a human catapult?" she said.

"No way," I told her. "You could get a bone fracture." You'd think she would've known that, with her dad being a doctor and everything.

Around four o'clock Rebecca's mom picked her up so they could take Fuzzby to the vet. Since I didn't have my big green book to read, I played double solitaire with Chirpy. I was just starting my sixth game when Mom knocked on my open door. "Annie?" she said, coming into the room before I'd even answered. I didn't know why she ever bothered with the knocking.

"Yeah?"

"Can you come set the table for me, sweetie? We're having meat loaf."

I hated meat loaf. "Okay, yeah. Just a second." I stacked a two of clubs on top of the ace and told Chirpy not to cheat. Then I went into the hallway, walking past Jared's room, where the door was shut tight just like it always was. The day after he died, Mom went in there and spent hours vacuuming and dusting and tidying and straightening, till the whole place was cleaner than an ice cube. I watched her do it. Then she closed the door and locked it. And that was that.

Mom was stirring things on the stove. "I haven't run the dishwasher yet," she told me without turning around. She must've had secret Mom-sense, because she always seemed to know whenever I entered a room even if she was looking the other way. "There should be plenty of plates in the cupboard, though."

I climbed up on the counter under the cupboard, even though Mom hated when I did that. But it was too much work to get a chair. There were exactly three plates left, the plastic ones that Mom called our "Not for Company Dishware." I grabbed the plates and put them on the table. One for me, Mom, and Dad. Then I went to get the napkins and the silverware.

"Thanks, hon," Mom said, turning around. "Don't forget to put out the—" And then she stopped talking and sucked in her breath real quick.

I turned to see what she was looking at, the plates on the table. It wasn't until I squinted my eyeballs that I saw it. Over at Dad's spot, on the far end of the table, I'd put down the plastic plate Jared made for Christmas in first grade, the one with the drawing of the lopsided Christmas tree that said "Hapy Holidayes!" in big orange letters.

"It was the only one left," I said, my voice soft as snow.

Mom didn't say anything, just walked quick over to the table and scooped the plate up and returned it to the cupboard with a soft clank. Then she went back to stirring peas on the stove and cleared her throat, deep and gargly. "There are some plates in the dishwasher, Annie," she said, not looking up. "You can wash one of those."

I didn't move right away. I just stood there, blinking. Because all of a sudden I was feeling squirmy inside, with a lump in my throat like I was in trouble. It was exactly the way I felt when I'd broken Mom's sewing machine last year, after she'd told me a million times not to use it. Only this time I wasn't sure why I felt like that, because setting the table like you were supposed to shouldn't make you a Huge Disappointment, Young Lady.

I took a plate out of the dishwasher, a regular white one, and I washed it with a sponge in the sink. "Mom?" I said, but she didn't answer. She just kept stirring the peas. I tried again. "Mom?"

"Yes, sweetie?" She didn't turn around.

"Are you mad at me?"

"Of course not, sweetie," she said, still stirring. "Why would I be mad?"

"Oh," I said. "Okay." But I wasn't sure I believed her.

When we finally sat down to eat, the peas were too mushy.

"Mom?" I said, after we'd been eating for a while with just forks and knives clanking, no talking.

She had a mouthful of peas. "Mmm-hmm?"

"Can I have my book back after dinner?"

She swallowed. "Oh, Annie . . . ," she said, looking over at my dad. He was ripping up a roll. "I don't think so, sweetie. I just don't think that's a good thing for you to be reading."

"But—"

"End of discussion," she said, and I knew that was that. I made my meanest squinty eyeballs at her, but she wasn't looking. "So," she said, and I could tell she was trying to be nice again. "What did you and Rebecca get up to today? Mrs. Harper said she saw you talking to the new neighbor."

I wondered for a second if Mrs. Harper had told my mom anything else, like that I'd taken her book. But I figured Mom would've been all bulging-eyeballs mad if she knew about the stealing, so probably Mrs. Harper hadn't figured it out yet. "Are you sure you cooked this long enough?" I asked her, poking the slab of meat loaf on my plate.

Mom didn't answer, just glanced at my dad, who was ripping up another bread roll.

"Because if you don't cook beef long enough," I said, "you can get *E. coli.*"

"Annie . . ."

"I mean, you have to be *really* careful, and cook it at an extra-hot temperature."

77
● ● ●

Mom licked her bottom lip, which is what she did when she was on the edge of being *supremely peeved.* "Annie Richards . . . ," she started. But I didn't care. I'd rather be in Hot Water, Missy, than die from a terrible disease.

"It's in that big green book," I said. "There's lots of super-important stuff like that. You'd know that if you read it, instead of hiding it."

Mom slapped her fork on the table so hard that Dad finally looked up from his dinner roll.

"Annie," he said, "don't argue with your mother." But I could tell he hadn't been listening at all.

Mom shook her head. "I don't appreciate your tone, young lady. And your dinner is fine. Now please start eating."

I pushed my plate away from me and didn't eat, just watched my parents chew without talking. Suddenly I wasn't hungry at all. As soon as Mom excused me from the table, I went upstairs and climbed under my covers. I didn't even finish my card game with Chirpy. I stayed in bed for a long time, just lying there, thinking about how loss of appetite was a sign of parasites. I needed that green book, so I could look it up, but I didn't know where it was.

When I finally heard Mom and Dad shut their door and go to bed, I pulled back my covers and tiptoed into Dad's office across the hall to search in the bottom drawer of his filing cabinet, because that's where Mom usually hid important stuff like Christmas presents. But the book wasn't there. It wasn't on the bookshelf, either. I was checking the desk drawers when I noticed Dad's calendar on the wall, with the red circle around July 9.

JARED'S B-DAY!!!

That's what it said.

And all of a sudden I thought of something so awful, it made my stomach churn inside me like clothes in a dryer. Even though Jared's birthday was coming up real soon, just one week away, he wasn't ever going to get any older. He would always be the exact same age he was in February.

But next year, on my birthday, I was going to turn eleven, and then the year after that I'd be twelve, and then I'd be older than my older brother.

I went back to my room and crawled under the covers, wondering which would be worse—growing older than Jared or catching the plague.

eight

● ● ●

Monday morning after Mom left for work and Dad started clacking away in his office, I went outside into the summer sunshine and strapped on all my bike gear—kneepads, elbow pads, helmet, and ankle bandages. After making sure my shoelaces were double knotted, I started out of the driveway. I needed to go to Lippy's to get vitamins. I'd seen a commercial on TV about how taking a multivitamin was an essential part of maintaining healthy overall body wellness. I'd spent all my allowance already, but I thought maybe Mr. L. would let me get them if I did sweeping or something.

But I'd barely made it out of my driveway when all of a sudden something dropped *splat!* down in front of me from the tree in Mrs. Finch's yard.

"SAFARI ATTACK!"

It was Doug Zimmerman, teeth showing sharp like a tiger's and his green bandanna covering his whole forehead and all of his hair. Only I didn't figure out any of that until I'd already had the bejeebers scared out of me so bad, I lost my grip on my handlebars and thudded right into the pavement.

"I got you!" Doug hollered, jumping up and down while I tried to wrestle my legs out from under my bike wheels. He pumped his fists in the air. "I saw you putting on your bike stuff, so I waited for you and planned my attack. That's what good safari ninjas do. Boy, I sure freaked you out, didn't I? Did you pee your pants?"

I hated Doug Zimmerman so much right then, I wanted to safari ninja him all the way to France. My butt was sore from the falling, and my arm, the right one, was prickly painful. I shifted my weight to look at it, and that's when I saw. The thick part of my lower arm, the underneath side that never got any suntan, was scraped up bad, about three whole inches wide. It was bright red with grainy white streaks and tiny pieces of gravel ground up under the skin. As soon as I saw that, it started to sting like I'd been jabbed with a cactus tree.

Doug bent down to look at it. "Oh, that looks sort of bad," he said. "Does it hurt?"

I whipped my head around and glared at him. "Of course it hurts!" I shouted. My breath was coming in huge giant gasps, and my chest was aching like I'd swallowed too much air. I watched as little beads of blood started to form on the surface of my skin. "I'm probably gonna get gangrene and they'll have to chop my arm off, and it's all your fault!" Gangrene was awful—I remembered that from the book. "I could even die, you know."

"Um." Doug took a couple steps back. "Annie, I don't think you're gonna die. It's just a scrape. Brad had his finger broken practically all the way off his hand one time and he didn't even—"

"Shut up!"

"Come on, get up already," Doug said. I didn't move, just stared at my arm. "I'm sorry I jumped at you, okay? You happy now?"

I kicked at my bike wheel, which just got my foot caught more. I wanted to tell Doug how much I hated him, but all that came out was a sniffle.

That's when I felt a hand on my shoulder, warm and firm.

"You okay, sweetie?" the voice said.

I swiveled my head to look over my shoulder. I thought, during the swiveling part, that it might be my mom, because she said things like "sweetie." But it didn't sound like Mom, and anyway she was at work.

It was white-haired Mrs. Finch. "I saw you crash," she said, nodding toward her window. "Looked terrible."

"It *was*," I said, and I glared at Doug. He stuck his hands in his pockets and kicked a pebble on the ground.

"I thought I'd come see if you were hurt. Oh my!" she exclaimed right then, and I could tell she'd just noticed my arm. "Oh dear, that must sting something fierce."

I felt the tears starting up behind my eyeballs. "It does," I said. And I didn't even care if I sounded like a baby. "And now I'm going to get gangrene, too."

"Well, we should get you home. I'm sure your parents will be able to clean you up and make you feel better."

I shook my head. "Mom's at work." My dad was home, clacking away at the computer in his office, but I knew he'd be no good. If I came home with a scraped-up arm, he'd just give me "Hello there, Moonbeam" and go back to clacking.

"Well then." I could see Mrs. Finch thinking about it. "I can help you get cleaned up if you like. I have some antibiotic cream. That will prevent any infection."

"Inside your house?" I asked.

She nodded.

I took a look at the haunted house and sniffled again. "Okay," I said.

"Good." She turned to Doug. "Young man, why don't you wheel that bike into my driveway and then karate-chop your way home before you get into any more trouble?"

Doug let out a tiny growl, but he picked up my bike, and Mrs. Finch helped me up, and we all walked together toward the haunted house.

I was climbing the steps to the front door when Doug called out to me, "You used to be fun, you know, Annie." I turned to look at him. His bandanna was drooping over one eyebrow. "But now," he said, "now you're just *careful*."

nine
● ● ●

While Mrs. Finch led me into her house, I kept my right arm elevated. That's what the big green book had said to do to keep your blood flowing normal after an injury. I tried to ignore how bad it was stinging, because that just got me thinking about gangrene and arm-chopping operations and dying. So instead I looked for ghosts.

I didn't see any. Mostly it was just boxes everywhere, big ones and little ones, with words scribbled on them. Lots of them said BOOKS or DINING ROOM, but there were other ones like KNICKKNACKS and TABLECLOTHS.

I thought that last one was weird, because why would you need a whole box of tablecloths, but I didn't say that to Mrs. Finch. I got the feeling she couldn't decide which box to unpack first, because they were all open, with stuff coming out every which way. There was only one that wasn't open yet. It was the big one I'd seen before, the one that said FRAGILE! in giant red letters. It was sitting lonely as a lost puppy on top of a table by the fireplace.

"Come on in here, sweetie," Mrs. Finch said, and she led me into the bathroom. I sat down on the lid of the toilet, and she dug through a cardboard box in the bathtub until she found what she was looking for. "Here we go," she said, holding up a yellow tube of something. "Now, let's just wash that scrape out thoroughly and we'll put some cream on it, and I think I have some large bandages, too. . . . Ah, yes, right here."

Mrs. Finch helped me careful careful peel off my elbow pad so it didn't touch my scrape, and then she cleaned my arm up, telling me exactly what she was doing while she was doing it. By the time she was done,

I figured we'd probably fought off any case of gangrene that might've been coming my way.

"There we go," she said, throwing the Band-Aid wrapper in the garbage. "That should just about do it, I think."

I patted the bandage down to make sure it was good and stuck. "Thanks, Mrs. Finch," I said.

She laughed. "Well, now, that's just not fair."

"What?" I squinted an eyeball at her. "What's not fair?"

"You know my name," she said, "but I don't know yours."

"Oh." I ran my left pointer finger around the edge of the Band-Aid. "It's Annie. Annie Zoë." Really my middle name was Emily, but I liked Zoë better.

"Well, it's nice to meet you, Annie Z."

"You too," I said.

She brushed off her old-lady slacks then, which were navy blue today. "So does your arm feel any better?"

I nodded. "A little. It still sort of stings, though."

She tilted her head and thought about that. "You

know, I might just have something for that, too."

"Really?" I said. I had no idea Mrs. Finch would have so much good fixing-up stuff. "What is it? More cream?"

"Follow me," she said.

We went to the kitchen, where there were even more boxes piled up everywhere. Mrs. Finch lifted two off the table and nodded to a chair. "Have a seat," she told me.

I sat.

Mrs. Finch started opening up her cupboards, pulling things out and putting them back—a box of spaghetti, a jar of olives, a can of tuna. When she didn't find what she was looking for, she started searching through the boxes stacked in front of the oven, pulling out more jars and bottles and cans and piling them on the floor. Finally she yelled out, "Aha!" and pulled out a small brass round thing with tiny holes all over it. It opened into two parts and had a tiny hook to make it close.

"What's that?" I asked.

"It's a tea infuser," she told me, standing up one creaky knee bend at a time. "For our tea."

"Oh." I crinkled my nose. "Actually, Mrs. Finch, I don't think I like tea very much."

"This is special tea," she told me. She set some metal containers down on the counter, six little squat ones, and then started digging around in a new box. "To make you feel better."

"Arm-scrape tea?" I asked.

"I guess you could call it that. Yes, arm-scrape tea. I like that." She pulled a pot out of the box and then filled it with water and put it on the stove. When she was all done, she sat down across from me at the table.

"It will be a few minutes," she told me.

"Okay," I said.

After that we stared at our hands for a while. And sometimes we'd take turns looking over at the stove, too, to check how the water was doing, I guess. Mostly it was just quiet.

Finally the water must've gotten hot enough, because Mrs. Finch stood up to fix the tea. She opened one of the tins and sniffed inside. Then she pinched out some stuff that looked like itty bitty twigs you'd find in an elf forest and dropped it into the infuser. She sniffed inside the other tins, too, and pinched out a little of this and a little of that, and when she was finished, she hooked the infuser shut and dropped it into a teapot that was bright blue with cherries on it. Then she poured in some hot water from the stove and put the lid on.

"We'll let that steep for a little bit," she said.

I just nodded, even though I didn't know what *steep* was. It sounded pretty funny though. I thought maybe Dr. Young would like it for his word wall.

Then we went back to staring at our hands again, which was even more boring than reading gardening magazines at the dentist's office. I was starting to think that Mrs. Finch didn't know how to talk to kids very well, because so far all she'd talked about was tea, so I figured it was up to me to do the talking. I tried to think up questions old people usually asked me.

Finally I had one.

"So," I said, "what's your favorite subject?"

I could tell Mrs. Finch wasn't expecting that one, because she coughed all surprised like.

"My favorite subject?" she said. "What do you mean?"

"Yeah, like math or science or spelling. Mine's social studies, because last year we studied the cuisine of the world's cultures, and Miss Kimball let us have a party with latkes and Swedish meatballs and cannolis and everything."

"Oh," Mrs. Finch said. She scratched her chin for a second and thought about it. "Well, I suppose my favorite subject would be philosophy."

"What's that?" I asked. "We don't have that one."

Mrs. Finch smiled. "No, I wouldn't guess you did. Philosophy is the study of knowledge and existence. Mainly it's a lot of thinking and asking questions."

"Who do you ask questions to?"

"Yourself mostly. You ask questions and think about what the answers might be. Usually you realize there aren't any answers."

"I think I'd rather eat meatballs."

Mrs. Finch laughed at that. She let out a big old-lady guffaw that just about shook the whole table. "You're something, Annie Z., you know that?"

After that Mrs. Finch checked the tea to see if it was ready. It was. She poured it into two teacups, one for me and one for her. They were both blue with cherries on them too, just like the teapot, and she had fancy saucers and everything. It almost felt like a tea party. She poured some milk in my tea, and a bit of sugar.

"So this will make my scrape feel better?" I asked her, holding the cup up to my lips. I didn't want to drink it yet. I was pretty sure it was going to taste awful.

Mrs. Finch sat down across from me and wrapped both hands around her teacup like she was getting warm in front of a fireplace. "Just take small sips," she said. "Savor it."

So I did what she said. I took a little tiny sip and swallowed. The tea was okay, not sweet like grape juice but not horrible like split pea soup. Across the table,

Mrs. Finch took a little tiny sip too.

I was going to drink some more but Mrs. Finch had set her cup down again, so I figured she really was taking her time like she said. I set mine down too and tried to think up more questions.

"What's your favorite color?" I asked.

It was lavender. I told her mine was yellow, and my second favorite was baby blue mixed with aquamarine.

Her favorite animal was sea lions. Mine was giraffes. Her favorite movie was *Casablanca*, which she said was old and black-and-white and very romantic. She tried to tell me what it was about, but it all sounded about as much fun as eating burned bread crusts.

"My favorite's *Captain Yorzo and the End of Time*," I said. "Me and Jared—that's my brother—we used to watch it in our pajamas in Mom and Dad's room on rainy days sometimes. Well, only once, but it was still our favorite."

"I've never heard of it."

"It's real good," I said. "Not boring at all. You probably wouldn't like it."

She smiled, then took the last sip of her tea. I noticed my cup was empty too.

"How did you like the tea?" she asked, walking to the counter and refilling her teacup.

"It was good," I said. "My scrape feels a little better, I think."

"See?" she said. "What did I tell you?" She held out the teapot. "Would you like another cup?"

"No, thank you," I said. "I mean, it's real good tea, but I think I should get going."

"Oh?"

"Yeah, I have to go to Lippy's."

"Who's Lippy?" she asked, sitting back down with her tea.

"It's the store at the bottom of the hill," I told her. "It's the best store there is. Mr. L. has everything. I'm going to get vitamins."

Mrs. Finch took a slow sip of tea. "Vitamins?"

"Mmm-hmm. They're an essential part of maintaining healthy overall body wellness. At least that's what they said on TV."

"You know, Annie Z.," Mrs. Finch said, looping a finger through the handle of her teacup, "vitamins can be dangerous if you don't know exactly which ones to take. It's best to talk to a doctor about it first."

"Really?" I twirled my teacup on the table. "The commercial didn't say anything about that." I wished I could look it up in my book. That'd be in there for sure. Then I snapped my head up to look at Mrs. Finch, because I had a really good idea. "You don't have a book called *The Everyday Guide to Preventing Illness*, do you? You have a lot of book boxes."

"I'm sorry, sweetie," she said. "I'm afraid I don't have that one."

"Oh. Well, you should get it maybe. It's really helpful for making sure you don't get sick and die. I used to have it, but I sort of lost it."

Mrs. Finch blinked at me a few times like she was going to say something, but she didn't right away, so I waited. "Actually," she said at last, "I think I may have an even better book for you."

"You do? Is it about vitamins?"

"Not exactly."

"Lyme disease?"

She drank the last of her tea. "You'll just have to wait and see, won't you? It's in one of my boxes. You up for a search?"

So Mrs. Finch and I went back to the living room, and she started poking around inside the boxes that said BOOKS on them. I searched too, even though I wasn't quite sure what we were looking for. When I found a book that looked old and important, I'd take it out of the box and hold it up, to see if maybe that was the right one, but Mrs. Finch just kept shaking her head.

"It's a short book," she told me, her head buried deep in a box. "You can probably read it all by yourself, although I'd be happy to help you with it if you like."

I had just finished up my third box, and was putting the books back inside it, when I noticed again the box that said FRAGILE! on the table across the room, with its top closed up tight and tape still around it. "Maybe it's in that one," I said.

Mrs. Finch looked up where I was pointing, and she shook her head quick. "No," she said. "It's not in there. I'm sure."

"Oh." I could sort of tell she didn't want to talk about it, but she was making me curious. "What *is* in that one?"

Mrs. Finch picked up three books from her box and set them down on the ground, one at a time, before she answered me. "Just some things I'm not ready to open yet," she said at last. Which was not actually an answer at all, but I figured that was probably the best I was going to get.

I was starting on a new box of books when all of a sudden Mrs. Finch cried out, "Aha! Here you go, Annie Z. Here's the book."

I scurried over quick to see, and she handed it to me. It was short, like she said. I looked at the title. And that's when I realized that Mrs. Finch might be bonkers.

"*Charlotte's Web*?"

She nodded. "I used to read it to my nephew all

the time. It's very good."

I'd heard about that one in school, and I was pretty sure it wasn't about diseases. I flipped through it. There were pictures of a goose, and a spider, and lots of ones of pigs. "You sure this is the right book?" I asked.

Mrs. Finch smiled. "I'm sure."

"Okay," I said, flipping through the pages again. At least the printing was a lot bigger than in the other one. "I'll try it. But I can stop if I want."

"It's a deal," she said.

ten

●●●

When I got home, I started reading right away, flopped down on my left side on the couch, so my arm scrape wouldn't get irritated against the couch fabric. But after three chapters it was becoming pretty clear to me that *Charlotte's Web* was a book about a pig. I tossed the book down on the floor.

I decided to go to Rebecca's house to ask Dr. Young about vitamins. Normally I would've ridden my bike, but even going turtle tracks you could never be sure about stupid safari ninjas jumping out of stupid trees. So I decided to walk. I still wore my Ace bandages, though, wound up tight around my ankles. Because you could get sprains just from walking, if you fell over or stepped the wrong way. And I checked the whole way for Doug Zimmerman hiding in trees, thinking about how dumb he was for saying I wasn't fun anymore. Of course I was fun. The careful sort of fun.

I rang the Youngs' doorbell and Rebecca answered. Her eyes were red and puffy and her nose was running.

"Do you have pollen allergies?" I asked her, stepping inside as she closed the door.

"No," she said. She wiped her nose.

"Well, what do you have then? You're not contagious, are you?"

Rebecca frowned at me. "You're late," she said, and she wiped her nose again. "Come on."

I didn't know what she was talking about, but she started walking through the house and out the sliding glass door to the backyard, so I followed her. Her babysitter, Tracey, was standing out there holding a shovel, and she didn't look too happy about it. Tracey never looked too happy about anything, though. She had dyed-black hair that was always pulled back in a tight tight ponytail, and she wore black makeup all around her eyes and the ugliest clothing I'd ever seen. Today she had on black jeans and a long-sleeved purple T-shirt that said I ♥ Dracula.

"Where's your dad?" I asked Rebecca.

"At work," she said, heading toward Tracey and the shovel. "We already dug the hole. We were just waiting for you before we buried him."

I stopped walking. My body felt like ice all over, all at that very second. "What?" I said. "What are you talking about?"

Rebecca turned around to look at me, her shoulders drooping. "Fuzzby," she answered. "We're burying him. Didn't you see my leaf? I left four messages, too." She sniffled. "I even went over to your house this morning, but your dad didn't know where you were."

Over by the fence, Tracey rapped her fingers on the handle of the shovel. "Are we going to do this or what, guys? I'm ready to go inside."

There was a hole in front of her, I noticed now, about a foot square and not too much deeper. And next to it was a box, a small one, Rebecca's box of 64 Crayola Crayons.

I took a step back. Fuzzby was in that box, I knew he was.

"He died?" I said, staring at the crayon box. My voice came out a whisper.

"Yeah," Rebecca said. I could see tears in the corners of her eyeballs. "When we took him to the vet yesterday, they said he was real sick, and this morning he was dead."

"Oh." I was sweating all of a sudden, like I'd been running in the Olympics, but I was still icy all over. Cold sweats was a bad sign, I remembered from the book, except I couldn't remember what it was a symptom of. Probably something awful.

"Guys?" Tracey called from the fence. "Hello? Are you ready yet?"

I put my hand up to my forehead. I thought I had a

fever, but I couldn't tell for sure. "I have to go home," I told Rebecca.

"What?" she said. "But we have to bury Fuzzby. I need your help, to make sure I do everything right."

"I can't." I shook my head. My eyes were still stuck like glue to that crayon box by the fence. "I can't."

"But—" Rebecca began, but Tracey cut her off.

"This is ridiculous," she said, rolling her eyes. "You two can figure it out yourselves. I'm going inside for some air-conditioning." And she dumped the shovel on the ground and walked back through the sliding door to the house.

Rebecca turned to look at me, sniffling and wiping her nose, and I knew she wanted me to stay worse than anything. But I couldn't do it.

"I have to go," I told her, shrugging my shoulders. "I'm sorry. I have to go home right now. I'm sick." And I raced around the house toward the side gate.

"You know what?" Rebecca called after me as I went, and she sounded mad, but I didn't look back. "I hope you *do* get sick! I hope you get *malaria!*"

The whole way home, every time I blinked, I could still see that crayon box behind my eyelids, and all I could think about was how Fuzzby was dead, just like Jared. I ran faster and faster, my feet pounding on the sidewalk. Dead, dead, dead, dead, dead.

As soon as I got home, I raced up the stairs two at a time and plugged the stopper in the upstairs bathtub, turning on the water full blast. Because I didn't know what the big green book would say about cold sweats, but I thought maybe cool water would be a good thing for it. When the water got high enough, I dunked myself inside, clothes and all, and I puffed out my cheeks and held my breath so I could get all my hair and my eyelashes and every last bit of me soaked. I pulled my head out and sat there for a long time, resting against the back of the tub, with the water dripping off my bangs and down my cheeks. And after a while my breathing went back to normal and I stopped seeing Fuzzby's crayon box behind my eyelids.

I drained the tub and got out, changing into new clothes and dumping my soggy ones in the washing machine. Then I switched all my Band-Aids—the one on my knee and the six on my legs and my stomach ones and even the big one from Mrs. Finch—because they'd gotten ruined in the tub. When I was done, I pulled back my wet hair into a ponytail, stuffed my feet into my alligator slippers, and went on a search to find my green book.

Dad was working in his office, but I already knew the book wasn't in there anyway. So instead I checked Mom and Dad's room. I looked in the closet, under the bed, and inside the dresser. It wasn't there. Then I checked the den, and the living room, and the kitchen. I even checked inside the freezer. It wasn't anywhere. I thought for a second that maybe Mom had locked it up inside Jared's room, because she knew I couldn't get in there. But then I remembered the look I'd seen on Mom's face when she shut Jared's door the day after he died—like she was shutting that door forever, for good. And I knew my book wasn't in there.

I decided that the only chance I had to make myself better was to read that pig book from Mrs. Finch.

Maybe if I kept going, there'd be something helpful. Like about asbestos poisoning or something.

I scooped the book off the floor by the couch, and I read the whole rest of the afternoon. I kept waiting for Rebecca to come over and tell me she was sorry for making me go to a surprise funeral and wishing I'd get malaria, but she never did. After dinner I walked over with my ankle bandages and my bike helmet, too, and left a leaf under her door as a signal that it would be okay for her to apologize, but she didn't call that entire night.

eleven
● ● ●

The next day was the Fourth of July, which meant the Junior Sunbirds had to do their Cedar Haven Community Summer Service Project. We did one every year, to raise money for something. I didn't ever really know what we were raising money for, but this year we were raising it by doing a Junior Sunbird car wash. Washing cars was not exactly something I liked very much. I could think of about fifty more fun things I'd rather be doing, and four of them involved math homework.

Dad drove me over right after breakfast. I sat in the

passenger seat in my ugly purple Sunbird outfit with my seat belt strapped tight around me, and I tugged at my arm-scrape Band-Aid. The new one I'd put on there wasn't quite as big as the one from Mrs. Finch, so part of the scrape showed on the sides, and I was worried it was going to get dirt inside and become infected. I should've put on two.

Dad pulled to a stop in the parking lot of Sal's Pizzeria, but he didn't turn off the car, just said, "Have fun, Moonbeam!" as I plopped myself onto the pavement. Then he drove off again, quick as a flash.

Right away I spotted Rebecca at the bake-sale table by the front door, so I went over to talk to her. She was standing next to Nadia Dwyer from school, and they were scooping brownies out of a Tupperware onto plates.

"Hey," I said when I got there.

Rebecca didn't look up. Nadia did, but as soon as she saw me, her eyes darted back to the brownies lickety-split. Which was weird, because me and Nadia had been aardvarks together in the school play last year, and Rebecca was my best friend in the whole world, and so I knew for a fact that neither one of them was deaf.

"How come you're not wearing your uniforms?" I asked them. Because they weren't. They were just wearing normal clothes—shorts and a T-shirt for Nadia and a red-and-white checkered dress for Rebecca.

Nadia rolled her eyes. *"Because,"* she said, and I knew just from the way she said it that no matter what came next was going to make me angry. "We weren't supposed to wear them. It's not a regular service project, it's a *car wash*, so Mrs. Harper didn't want us to ruin our outfits. She called all the parents last night to tell them."

"She didn't call mine," I said.

Nadia licked a crumb of brownie off her thumb. "Oh," she said. "Well, too bad for you, I guess. What the heck happened to your arms, anyway?" Nadia asked, pointing to my Band-Aids. Rebecca still didn't look up, just went on scooping.

"Rebecca—" I started, but Nadia cut me off.

"Rebecca's mad at you," she said. "She told me so. That's why she's not talking to you. She's mad at you because you didn't care when Fuzzball died—"

"Fuzzby," Rebecca said, cutting an extra-large brownie in half with a plastic knife.

"Right, Fuzzby. Anyway," Nadia said to me, "you didn't care about Fuzzby, so Rebecca doesn't care about you."

"But that's not fair," I said. Because it wasn't. "I had to go home. I was sick."

Rebecca took the last brownie out of the Tupperware and shut the lid with a *woopft*. Nadia just shrugged.

"I was sick," I said again. "And I didn't even have my book about diseases to check things, either. I only had the book Mrs. Finch gave me, which isn't even helpful at all." I didn't know why I was still talking, except that I was sort of hoping that if I talked enough, maybe Rebecca would talk back. But she didn't. She started laying out cupcakes.

Nadia plucked a brownie off the table and stuck it in her mouth, even though I was almost positive she didn't pay fifty cents for it like she was supposed to.

● ● ●

"Who's Mrs. Finch?" she asked me.

I tugged at the bottom of my Junior Sunbird sash, the one with only three badges on it. "She's the old lady who moved into the haunted house," I said. "I was over there drinking arm-scrape tea and—"

"You went over to the haunted house?"

That surprised me, because it wasn't Nadia who said it. It was Rebecca.

"Yeah," I said, glad Rebecca was finally talking to me again. "She's pretty nice, actually, only she—"

"You went over there without me?" Rebecca's arms were folded across her chest, and her eyebrows were scrunched-up angry. "You went inside and you didn't even *tell* me?"

"Well, yeah, but . . ." I was starting to get squirmy, and sweaty under the armpits. I wondered if that meant I had tuberculosis or it was just from wearing my stupid Junior Sunbird outfit in the hot sun. "I was going to tell you when I went to your house," I said. "But you were all freaked out and stuff, so I didn't get a chance."

Rebecca glared at me. "I was not freaked out," she said, and I wanted to say that yes she was, plus she looked sort of freaked out at that moment, but I didn't. "I was *sad*. I was sad because of Fuzzby."

"Yeah," Nadia said, shoving the last of the brownie into her mouth. "If you were a good friend, you'd know that." And she linked elbows with Rebecca, like *they* were best friends, which I happened to know for a fact that they were *not*.

"Yeah," Rebecca said.

And that made me madder than anything. "Fuzzby was just a hamster," I said. My words came out so sharp, you could've chopped carrots with them. "He didn't even do anything but poop anyway. It's not like it matters. It's not like your brother died."

Rebecca's mouth dropped open when I said that, and so did Nadia's.

"And just so you know," I told Rebecca, "I probably do *not* have malaria, so it looks like your wish didn't even come true about that." And I walked away with a stomp that would've been nice and loud if I wasn't wearing my stupid dress shoes with the soft plastic bottoms that weren't good for stomping.

Right at that moment Mrs. Harper called us over to form a circle and do the Sunbird salute. I got there first, and she wrapped me up in a hug.

"You did bring some street clothes, didn't you, Annie?" she said as she pulled back to look at me.

"No," I said, shaking my head. "I didn't know I was supposed to."

"Oh." She raised an eyebrow. "I talked to your father last night, but I suppose he forgot to mention it. That's all right. You can work at the bake-sale table so you won't get your uniform wet. I'm sure Nadia and Rebecca will be happy to have the help."

"No!" I said. It came out a lot louder than I wanted it to, which sort of made it sound like I was being attacked by the Loch Ness monster. "Sorry," I said, softer. I looked over at Rebecca and Nadia, who were almost all the way to the circle, still with their arms linked. "I mean, I want to wash cars."

"Okay," Mrs. Harper said. "That's fine, Annie. You

can wash cars if you want."

"Thanks." I went to go stand next to Sue Beth McKernin in the circle, but Mrs. Harper stopped me.

"Annie?" she said.

"Yeah?"

"I've been meaning to ask you. You don't remember what I did with Mr. Harper's book, do you? The green one we were looking at the other day? He's been searching for it, and I can't seem to find it anywhere."

I gulped. "No," I said, shaking my head fast. "Don't remember. Sorry."

She shrugged. "Well, I'm sure it'll turn up sooner or later, don't you think?" The way she was looking at me right then, like her eyeballs were squinty little laser probes, I thought for a second that she must've known I was the one who stole it. But she didn't say anything else, just gave me one last giganto hug and called the Sunbirds to order.

Sue Beth gave me a friendly smile when I went to stand next to her, which was nice because across the circle Rebecca and Nadia were both sticking their

tongues out at me. I tried to ignore them while we
started up the "Welcome Fellow Sunbirds" song.

> Welcome fellow Sunbirds
> We're glad to have you here
> It's nice to have the Sunbirds
> To help me through the years

Jared always called it "Welcome Fellow Dumb
Birds," and once when I was all dressed up for a troop
meeting, he even made up his own words to it.

> Welcome fellow dumb birds
> We're glad that we are dumb
> Our outfits look so stupid
> And our cookies taste like scum

I'd been real mad when he sang that one, his voice
all high and squeaky. But I was starting to think that it
was actually a pretty good version after all.

twelve

●●●

When we were finished with the singing and the official Sunbird announcements, Mrs. Harper split us up into groups. I went over to the side of the parking lot with the washers and we started filling up buckets with hose water.

Jessica and Tanya were in charge of suds. They were best-friends-forever and also kind of mean, so no one ever argued when they said stuff. That's why they got the bright blue sponges shaped like giant dog bones and buckets of soapy water, and Sue Beth and I got stuck with the hoses. It could have been worse, though, because at least we got to blast things with water. Kate had to do drying, which was the worst job there was, but she was the nicest of anyone, so she got stuck with it. Also her mom said she'd help.

While we were hosing, me and Sue Beth played I'm going on a picnic, except instead of picnic we said Mars, because that was more fun. Sue Beth was the county spelling bee champion for our grade last year, so she knew tons of good words. Except I don't think she knew what all of them meant.

"I'm going to Mars," I said as I sprayed a car, "and I'm going to bring an abalone shell, a banana, a cataract, a dog, an enzyme, a fish, a guerrilla warfare, a hat, an iris, and . . ." I worked hard clearing off some suds while I thought up a word for *j*. "And a joke."

"A joke?" Sue Beth asked. She had lots of pretty curly brown hair, and it was pulled back with a pink polka-dot headband. I wished I had a polka-dot headband.

"Yeah," I said. "I bet you'd need a lot of jokes if you went to Mars. So you'd be able to tell them to the aliens and crack 'em up."

We played the Mars game three times. Only once we did Jupiter. And we sprayed cars with water and I did *not* look at Rebecca and Nadia, way over by the sidewalk, with their stupid bake-sale table. I was getting pretty wet from the water spraying off the cars on me. My ugly purple skirt was sticking to my legs, and my socks with the ugly green tassels looked like something Mr. Normore's wiener dog puked up. And all my Band-Aids on my arms and legs were soaked again and the edges were starting to curl. Everyone else was wet, too, but they were all wearing normal clothes so they didn't look so dumb.

Sue Beth and I were just refilling the buckets for Tanya and Jessica, deciding if we should take a picnic to Saturn, when I saw who was next in line.

It was Doug Zimmerman. On his bicycle. He grinned at me, mouth wide open like a jack-o'-lantern.

"Hello, Aaaaaannie," he said.

I just kept on filling up the bucket and pretended I didn't even see him. I was still mad at him for safari ninja-ing me and almost giving me gangrene and saying I wasn't fun anymore.

He pedaled forward in the car-wash line until he was real close to me. His bike tires were making sudsy tracks all over the parking lot, so you could tell exactly where he'd been. "Aw, Annie, you're not still mad at me, are you? I said I was sorry about ninja attacking you. How's your arm?"

Doug Zimmerman didn't care one ant's behind how my arm was, and I knew it. "What do you want?" I said.

"Are you going to the picnic tonight?" he asked. "Because we're going to build the best obstacle course *ever*. Aaron got about a billion pool noodles 'cause he's been lifeguarding all summer, and we're going to use them as limbo lines. Also maybe pole vaulting. And then when you get to the last part of the obstacle course, in the lake, you have to tightrope walk on the noodles. I've been practicing at the pool. It's real hard." He looped a figure eight. "So? You coming?"

I sprayed suds off the car in front of me and didn't look at Doug. "You're not supposed to horse around in the pool," I said. "You could drown."

"I think the obstacle course sounds fun," Sue Beth said, but I glared at her and she went back to hosing.

"You should both come," Doug said. "I invited other people from school too. We're gonna have a contest."

Someone in line behind him honked a horn.

"Get out of the way," I told Doug. "We're trying to wash cars."

Doug looped another lazy circle. "Well, what if I want a bike wash?" he said.

"This isn't a bike washing place, Doug," I said. "It's a Junior Sunbird *car* wash. And you didn't even pay. So go away."

"Yeah," Sue Beth said. "Go away or we'll hose you."

I decided right then that if Rebecca really wanted to be mad at me for good, I was going to make Sue Beth my new best friend. I liked the way she thought.

Doug put his feet flat on the ground. "Nope," he said. "I want a bike wash. And you should give me one for free. It's a community service project, and I'm in the community."

"Okay," I said, and I turned to Sue Beth when I said it. "I guess if you really want a bike wash . . ."

I think maybe Sue Beth was my brain twin or something, because she figured out what I meant right away. We both put our thumbs on our hoses so they sprayed real powerful, and we shot the water right at Doug. We did some screaming and shouting too.

Doug wasn't mad like I wanted him to be, though. He put his arm up in the air and pretended to scrub in his armpit like he was taking a shower. I guess that was pretty funny, and Sue Beth and I started laughing at that and spraying him more, and Doug kept taking his pretend shower.

But then Jessica and Tanya saw us, and they must've wanted to help Doug's bike wash too, because they ran over and started rubbing his bike all over with their soapy sponges. Kate's mom got mad and started yelling, angry like a hornet, and Sue Beth and I stopped with the hoses right away, but Jessica and Tanya kept going. They soaped Doug's bike all up, and then they started soaping him. They soaped his sneakers and his shorts and his T-shirt, even his hair. I could tell Doug didn't like the soaping very much. He tried to get away, but Tanya grabbed his bike handle and wouldn't let him.

"There's soap in my eyes!" Doug started hollering. "There's soap in my *eyes*!" He tried to wipe at his eyeballs with his hands, but they were soapy too.

That's when I remembered I had a hose. "I'll help!" I shouted at him. Because if you got a foreign object in your eye, you were supposed to wash it out right away, or you could go blind. So I sprayed him, right in the eyes. But I guess he wasn't ready for it, because the spray knocked him over on his butt, bike and everything. And even though he was a boy, he started crying.

"Girls!" Mrs. Harper came running over, her elbows jiggling like Jell-O, and she looked angrier than a cat in a bathtub. "What's going on?" she asked. Rebecca and Nadia were right behind her. "What happened?" She helped Doug off the ground.

"The girls attacked him," Kate's mom said. "They just started spraying water at this poor boy."

I could tell Kate's mom had never met Doug

Zimmerman before, because she called him a "poor boy" instead of an idiotic tree jumper.

"She started it," Jessica said. And she was pointing at me. Her and Tanya's sponges were on the ground, like they hadn't done anything wrong at all.

"Did not!" I shouted.

"Annie," Mrs. Harper said, "I'm very disappointed in you. This is not the way Junior Sunbirds behave." She frowned at me, and I got the feeling that she thought Not Acting Like a Junior Sunbird was worse than punching puppies. I bet if she really knew about the book stealing, she would've kicked me out of the troop for sure. "Now I want you to apologize to Doug, and then I'm going to help him get cleaned up."

"Sorry, Doug," I said, the water still whooshing out of my hose onto the pavement, splashing up onto my socks.

Nadia smiled at me with a not-very-nice look on her face. "Good thing you're not friends with her anymore, huh?" she said to Rebecca, and not even quiet either. "She's crazy."

That's when I sprayed her. Just to show her how crazy I was. She screamed loud as a fire truck, but I didn't care, I just soaked her, toes to hair. And I sprayed Rebecca, too, for standing right next to Nadia and letting her be mean and not even saying anything.

"Annie!" Mrs. Harper screeched, shocked all over. "That is *not* the way Junior Sunbirds beha—"

But she didn't get to finish her sentence, because I soaked her too.

Then, while they were all busy dripping and screaming and thinking what a crazy loon I was, I ran into Sal's Pizzeria and locked myself in the toilet stall. I didn't leave until the pizza lady came in fifteen minutes later and said my dad was there to pick me up.

I unlocked the door and trudged out of the bathroom, making sopping-wet footprints the whole way. Dad just stood there, shaking his head slowly side to side. I thought he was going to say something about me being a soaking mess, or getting into trouble, or maybe even being a lunatic, but all he said was "Come on, Moonbeam. Let's go home."

thirteen

●●●

As soon as I opened the front door, Mom called out, "Annie?" from the den, and I knew that meant I had to go in and talk to her. Dad went straight up to his office to work, which I thought was pretty smart of him, because even from two rooms away I could smell the Lemon Pledge fumes. When Mom was upset about something, she cleaned. The week after Jared died, I bet we had the cleanest house on the planet, with vacuum lines running over every inch of the carpet.

I walked to the den, still wet in my ruined soggy purple Junior Sunbird outfit.

"Um," I said from the doorway. I didn't go all the way inside. Mom was polishing our coffee table so hard, I was surprised there was any of it left. I just knew I was going to get it for the hosing. I was going to be grounded, or lose my TV privileges, or have to be on dish duty for a week. "Hey."

Mom put down her polishing rag. "Hey, Annie." Her voice came out nicer than I expected. "Come here, sweetie."

I was surprised by the "sweetie." I wondered if it was some sort of trap, but I didn't have much choice but to go on over.

Mom wrapped me up in a hug, squeezing me so tight, I thought maybe the polishing fumes had been getting to her brain. The big green book had mentioned something about that. But she didn't look like she was having hallucinations or anything, so I figured she was probably okay. She patted the couch with her hand, and we both sat down, my skirt pressing itchy wet wrinkles into the backs of my legs.

"So," she said, looking at me right in the eyeballs.

But then she didn't say anything else. Which after a while made me feel sort of squirmy and wonder about the fumes again.

"Um, Mom?" I said. "Didn't you want to yell at me or something?"

She smiled a tiny little smile. "No," she said, and she shook her head. "It's just . . . I'm worried about you, I guess."

"You are?" I thought that was weird. I wasn't the one acting kooky. "How come?"

"Well, it's just this whole thing today was so *unlike* you, Annie. You're normally so well-behaved, and then you go and spray down everyone at the car wash. It's a bit worrisome."

I sighed. "I wasn't being a very good Sunbird, I guess." I figured if I sounded sorry about it, maybe Mom wouldn't give me dish duty. But also I was starting to think that maybe I really *wasn't* a very good Sunbird. Maybe that's why I only had three badges. If they had badges for book stealing and making your best friend hate you and soaking half your Sunbird troop, I'd have a whole sash full already. I wondered if Mrs. Harper was going to kick me out. It would probably serve me right.

"But there are other things I'm worried about, too," Mom said. "And I just thought . . . well, I thought it was time for us to talk about them."

I watched a drop of water drip slowly off my skirt onto the floor. "Like what?" I asked.

"Well . . ." Mom lifted up my left arm and gently tapped each one of my soggy Band-Aids—the ones for the just-in-case poison oak spots, and the two that were covering up places I thought I might have sun poisoning. "And that book you were reading, with all the diseases."

"*The Everyday Guide to Preventing Illness*?" I said.

She nodded. "That's the one." Then she sighed, real big and deep. "And Mrs. Harper tells me you've been overly concerned about sunblock, and Mr. Normore saw you walking down the street last night wearing your bike helmet." She tucked a piece of hair behind my ear. "Annie, honey, I just think you're worrying too

130
● ● ●

much. You need to stop."

I thought about that, and then I shook my head. "No. I don't think so."

"Excuse me?" Mom said, raising up one eyebrow.

"I don't think I've been worrying too much," I told her. "I think it's good to be careful."

"But—"

"*You're* the one who said I should wear sunscreen when I'm outside. And you bought that bike helmet for me too, when I first got my bike."

"That's true, Annie, but this is different."

"How?"

Mom started licking her bottom lip then, and I thought for a second I really was going to get dish duty. But in the end all she said was "There's a line, Annie. There are things you should be worried about, and things you shouldn't. Besides"—she straightened the magazines on the coffee table—"all you really need to be worried about is being a kid, and being happy. Let your father and me worry about the other stuff, all right?"

I knew for a fact that wasn't going to work. Because

Mom and Dad didn't know all the stuff to worry about like I did.

"Can I have my book back?"

"Annie," Mom said, "I want you to tell me one thing that you're happy about, right at this moment."

"Then can I have my book back?"

"No." She smoothed out my Junior Sunbird sash. "Go on. One happy thing."

I glared at her for a second, but she wasn't giving in, so finally I closed my eyes and tried to think. Mostly what I thought about was how drippy and itchy I was, and how I really wanted to not be wearing my ugly wet Junior Sunbird outfit anymore so I didn't get a horrible rash, but that was not a happy thing, and I knew I wasn't going to get to change clothes until I came up with one. So I thought some more.

Finally I had it.

"Ducks," I said, and I opened my eyes.

Mom tilted her head to one side. "Ducks?" she asked.

"Yeah. The ducks at the lake. It's a happy thing

because today we get to go down and feed them, just like we used to do with Jared. I've been saving up the bread, remember? I'm going to get at least fifty points this year."

Mom didn't say anything, so I thought maybe that wasn't a happy enough thing and I needed to keep going. So I thought of some more stuff.

"And fireworks," I said. "Fireworks are good too." Actually, now that I was thinking about it, there were lots of happy things today. Ducks, fireworks, hot dogs, watermelon. For being a holiday without any presents in it, the Fourth of July was a pretty good one. "Remember how when Jared was little he used to think the fireworks were for his birthday, because they were right in the same week?" I smiled, thinking about it.

But Mom wasn't smiling. She was frowning hard, picking lint off her sweater.

I watched three more drips fall to the floor from my soggy skirt, waiting for Mom to tell me I'd come up with some good happy things and I could go change, but she didn't. So finally I said, "Mom? Can I go now?"

She snapped her head up quick to look at me, like she'd forgotten I was there. "Oh," she said. "Yes, of course."

I stood up. "What time are we leaving, anyway?" I asked.

"Leaving?"

"For the lake. What time are we going?"

Mom went back to picking at her sweater, even though I didn't see any lint balls there at all, and I had twenty-twenty eyesight, I knew that for a fact.

"Mom?"

"I think I'm going to sit out the Fourth of July this year, sweetie," she said.

"What?" You couldn't sit out the Fourth of July. It was a holiday. With hot dogs.

"I'm sorry," she said, standing up and giving me a kiss on the forehead. "I'm just not feeling up to it. But if you want to go, I'm sure your father will take you."

"But I don't want to go with just Dad," I said. "We used to go all together. Me and you and Dad and Jare—"

"I want you to take off those Band-Aids when you change, all right?" Mom said, picking up her polishing rag. "All of them. From now on you are not allowed to put on a Band-Aid unless you are actually bleeding, you understand me?"

I sighed as I headed for the door. I turned around to say Mom wasn't being fair, but she was back to polishing, the exact same spot she'd been cleaning when I came in.

fourteen

●●●

I peeled off all my Band-Aids careful slow—off
my arms and my knees and my legs and everywhere—
each one pulling my skin with a painful pinch at the
end. I didn't want to take them off, but when Mom
came in to vacuum my floor, she said I didn't have a
choice young lady. I got to keep the one on my arm
scrape, though, even though the scrape wasn't bleeding, because when I tucked up the corner to show her
underneath, what with the yellow goo just starting to
form a scab, she made a grossed-out face and said I
could leave it on. Also I kept the four on my toes for the

athlete's foot, because Mom didn't know about those ones, and I didn't plan on telling her.

As soon as she finished with the vacuuming, I dove under my bed to find my Band-Aid box, but it turned out there weren't any left in it. I dumped the box in the trash can and went downstairs to pack the cooler for the lake. Even if Mom wasn't coming, I wasn't going to have a bad Fourth of July.

I lugged the watermelon out of the fridge, and all the cans of orange soda we had, and shoved them inside the cooler. Then I opened up the bread box to get out the bread for the ducks.

It was empty.

"Dad!" I hollered. "Dad! Where's the bread?"

Dad popped his head into the kitchen, holding a folded-up magazine. "What's that, Moonbeam?" he asked.

"Where did the bread go?"

"Oh." He shook his head. "It was all stale, so I threw it away."

"Dad! I was saving that. For the ducks. I *told* you."

He checked his watch. "Sorry, Moonbeam. I guess I forgot. You about ready to go?"

"I guess," I grumbled. "Let me just get something." I went upstairs and found the pig book, shoved under a pile of blankets at the foot of my bed. I figured if I wasn't going to have Jared or my mom or the ducks to keep me company, I might as well bring something to do.

By the time we got to the lake, all the good grassy spots by the water were taken, so Dad and I set up our blanket and chairs over by the snack stand.

"Can I have some money?" I asked Dad. "I want to get food."

Dad dug ten dollars out of his pocket and handed it to me without looking up from his magazine.

"Thanks."

Usually Mom said two hot dogs was the limit, but I figured Dad wouldn't care how many I ate, so I was going to get four. But while I was waiting in line, I started to think about the chapter in the big green book about food poisoning. By the time I got to the front of the line, I had folded the ten-dollar bill into a tiny square and unfolded it five times, thinking hard.

"Can I help you?" the man inside the snack stand asked me.

I looked at his fingers. They were a little grimy under the nails.

"Who cooks the hot dogs?" I asked him. "Do you do it?"

He pointed his thumb over his shoulder. "Jimmy's at the grill tonight. How many you want?"

"What temperature do you cook them at?"

"Huh?" he asked.

"How hot is the grill?"

He wrinkled his forehead. "It's a grill," he said. "It's hot."

"But *how* hot?" I leaned my head over to try to see past the snack stand to the grill behind. "Is Jimmy wearing gloves? How long has the meat been out? What's the expiration date?"

He put his elbows up on the counter. "You want a hot dog or not, kid?"

I sighed. The hot dogs smelled barely burned on the sides, just the way I liked them, but food poisoning could kill you. "No," I said. "Thanks." And I slumped back over toward our spot on the blanket.

I was halfway there when I felt a poke in my back.

"Hey, Aaaaaannie." It was Doug Zimmerman. He was holding a cardboard box with six hot dogs inside, and all of them were one-hundred-percent covered in ketchup.

"Hey," I said, and I kept on walking.

"I'm not mad about you hosing me," Doug said, walking quick after me. "Just so you know."

"You're not?"

"Nah. I figure now we're even from when I ninja attacked you."

I thought about that. It sounded pretty fair to me. "Okay," I said.

I kept on walking, but Doug blocked me with his foot, so I had to stop or I'd crash right into him. "Hey, you want to know what I did with that badger?" he asked me.

"What badger?"

"The one from Mrs. Harper's yard sale. You wanna know what I did with it?"

"Not really."

"I stuck it in Trent's closet!" Doug said. "Way up high on the top shelf. And it's leaning out far, too, so the next time Trent opens his closet door, it'll fall on him."

"Okay," I said, trying to pass him. But Doug blocked me again. I had to step back quick so his hot dogs didn't mash into my shirt and make me all ketchupy.

"And I glued shark teeth in its mouth, too," he told me. "Like fangs. It's real scary. And down at the bottom where it said 'Badger'? I changed it. Now it says 'Evil Badger of Doom.' Trent's gonna pee his pants for sure."

"That's great, Doug. Really," I said. "Now can you let me go? I have stuff to do."

"What sort of stuff?"

"I have a book to read."

Doug wrinkled his nose. "That's boring. Why don't

you come do the obstacle course with us? Aaron helped us set it up real good." He pointed toward the far end of the grass, where the big rocks jutted into the lake. "Rebecca's there too. There's lots of kids from school."

I looked, and sure enough, there were half the kids from our class, Rebecca and Nadia and Sue Beth too. They were attacking each other with pool noodles, and splashing in and out of the water doing a crab walk. Everyone was laughing and shrieking so hard, you could probably hear them from outer space. I wouldn't have gone over there if someone paid me.

"No thanks," I said to Doug. "Looks too dangerous."

"It is not," he said, and I could tell by the way he rolled his eyes that he was feeling the way that Dr. Young liked to call *exasperated*. "It's totally fine. Anyway"—he grabbed one of the hot dogs out of the box and took a big bite, munching with his mouth open so I could see all the pieces as he chewed—"you do dangerous stuff all the time."

"No I don't," I said.

"Do too. You go in the car with your parents, for one thing. That's dangerous, 'cause you could get in a car accident. And even just eating lunch you could choke on a sandwich or something."

"Shut up," I told him. "You don't even know what you're talking about." But he was right, and I knew it. Cars and eating *were* dangerous. "But . . ." I said, trying to think things out, "that's different, though. Because you have to do that stuff—you don't have a choice. You just need to be careful when you do it. Like wearing a seat belt, and chewing all the way. But obstacle courses"—I looked over across the grass, where Rebecca was dodging Aaron's Super Soaker and screaming—"there's no reason to do that at all."

Doug put the rest of the hot dog back in the box and swallowed. He was looking at me like I was a nut job. "You do it 'cause it's fun, Annie," he said. And he shrugged his shoulders and walked away.

For the next hour or so Dad and I sat around waiting for the sun to go down, Dad reading his magazine and me reading *Charlotte's Web*. We drank orange soda and nibbled on watermelon without talking, while everyone around us laughed and shouted and played music and ran around looking like they were having a lot more fun than we were. I wished I had the bread for the ducks. I wished my mom were there. I wondered what happy things she'd think up if I asked her. They'd be all about vacuuming, probably. I sighed and turned a page in my book.

After a while the sky got so dark that I had to squint my eyes to read. I looked over at Dad, who had set his magazine down beside him on the blanket and was staring at a swarm of gnats. I wondered for a minute if he might like playing the picnic game, but I never opened my mouth to ask him. Instead I just traced my pointer finger over the picture of the animals on the front of my book, over and over, covering every single line, until the sky finally turned a deep blue-black, and everyone got whisper quiet. That's when the fireworks started up.

I lay on my back on the blanket, my bare toes tickling a patch of grass, and I watched the sky over the lake light up all different colors. Then, after a while, I closed my eyes and I just listened. Everyone around me was oohing and ahhing, every time the fireworks popped, but I didn't need to look anymore.

Last year it had been all of us, me and Mom and Dad and Jared. All of us together, sitting on our blanket like usual, right up close to the water. And I'd been busy watching the fireworks when all of a sudden, in the middle of a big-kazam loud one, Jared caught me off guard and dumped a handful of grass right on my head. So I waited until I knew he wasn't expecting it, and then I pretended to be looking at the sky, but really I was grabbing at the grass next to me, and when I had a good chunk I stuffed it down his shirt. And then he got me back with grass in my socks. After that there was some chasing but finally we decided to call a truce and we snuggled up next to Mom and Dad under the extra blanket, all of us together cozy warm, and watched the rest of the show. And then, just after the last firework had gone off but right before everyone started clapping, in that second of quiet, Jared turned to look at me and I thought he was going to shove grass in my socks again but he didn't. He just grinned real big and said, "That was fun, huh?"

I wished there was a way to keep that in a bottle, that one moment of wonderful perfect, so I could open it up whenever I needed to get a good whiff.

When the fireworks were all over, I opened my eyes and stared up into the black sky speckled with stars and firework dust. Everyone started rustling around, picking up their stuff and heading back to their cars. I wanted to stay there forever, stretched out on the grass in the dark with just the hint of a breeze.

"You coming, Moonbeam?" Dad asked.

I sighed big and sat up, shoving the last of the watermelon back in the cooler.

There were a million and a half cars leaving the lake, so Dad had to drive about an inch per minute slow, which made me glad because what Doug had said about car accidents was making me extra worried. I decided right then that I was going to wear my helmet whenever we drove somewhere. I twisted against my seat belt to watch the boats on the lake as we drove by, and I got to thinking. Mostly what I was thinking about was how, between the hosing at the car wash and having to take off all my Band-Aids and the ducks and the hot dogs and everything, it had been the worst Fourth of July in the history of the universe. And the more I got to thinking, it all got to making me mad.

"Dad?" I said finally, when we were just a block from home.

"Yes, Moonbeam?"

"Why didn't you tell me about the uniforms?"

"What's that?" He kept his eyes on the road as we turned the corner.

"Why didn't you tell me I didn't have to wear my stupid Sunbird outfit today at the car wash? Mrs. Harper called you and told you, and you didn't even say anything."

"Sorry, Moonbeam," he said, slowing down to pull into our driveway. "I guess I must have forgotten."

He stopped the car and turned the engine off, plowing outside before I had a chance to say anything else. I followed him into the house and found my mom coming down the stairs with a basket of laundry.

"Hey there," she greeted us as Dad closed the front door. "How were the fireworks?"

I gave her an eyeball glare so fiery hot it could've toasted marshmallows. "They were *fine*," I said. "You would know that if you'd been there."

Dad glanced at my mother and then looked at me. "Now, Moonbeam . . . ," he said. I swiveled on my heel and gave him the eyeball glare too.

"Don't call me Moonbeam anymore," I told him.

"What?" he said.

"Don't call me that anymore unless you mean it."

Mom came down the last few steps. "Annie, are you okay?" she asked. "What's going on?"

I shook my head at them, at both of them. "You still have to be my parents, you know. Even if Jared's dead. You still have to be my parents." And then I bolted past my mom up the stairs and into my room, slamming my door closed behind me.

Ten minutes later I was stretched out on my bed

with my arms over my face when there was a quiet tap on my door, and Mom peeked her head inside my room. "Annie?" she said, wispy-quiet. I didn't answer.

She opened the door all the way and walked softly softly over to my bed, sitting on the edge beside me. "We're trying, you know," she said. She took a long, deep breath. "Your father and I. We're really trying."

I didn't say anything, just stared at the inside crook of my elbow. I had a headache, right at the front of my brain, and I was thinking it was probably a migraine.

After a few minutes Mom stood up and gave me a peck on the forehead, then left my room as quiet as she'd come in, shutting the door as she went.

When the door clicked closed against the latch, I turned to look at it.

"Try harder," I said. But it just came out a whisper.

fifteen

●●●

The next morning I still had that headache, and my stomach was a little bit queasy too. So after I watched Mom drive off in her car for work, and Dad was busy clacking in his office, I went on another search for the big green book.

I searched for an hour and a half almost, in the weirdest spots I could think of—at the bottom of the recycle bin, behind the television, underneath the fern in the den. Finally I found it, behind a stack of towels in the upstairs linen closet. I yanked it out and went to my room to read.

It turned out there were about a million things I might have, the flu or a concussion or Colorado tick fever or even mono. But I was pretty positive that out of all of them, I had Ebola. And wouldn't you know, there was no cure for that one. It was all rashes and bleeding, and then you just up and died, and no one could save you.

In the meantime, I needed more Band-Aids. I strapped on my helmet, wrapped up my ankles good and tight, and headed down to Lippy's, just walking.

Mr. L. wasn't there. It was only Tommy behind the counter, playing a video game on a little gray machine like the one Jared used to have, that beeped and buzzed every three seconds. I went to the Band-Aid aisle and plucked a box off the shelf.

"Two eighty-three," Tommy said when he rang me up.

"Um"—I straightened a stack of breath mints on the counter—"actually, I don't have any money."

Tommy shut the cash register drawer with a clang. "Now I have to do a void," he said.

"But I can do sweeping," I said, really quick. "And then instead of paying me for that you can just give me the Band-Aids."

He was scribbling numbers on a slip of paper beside the register. "We don't do that," he said without looking up. "We only do money."

"But what if—"

"You have to talk to my dad when he gets back."

"When's that?"

Tommy shrugged. "Twenty minutes? He just left to get change."

"You think he'll give me the Band-Aids then, if I do sweeping?" I asked.

"Probably not."

"Oh." I sighed. "Hey, Tommy?"

"Yeah?"

"Do you know any good doctors I can ask a question about vitamins? I need to start taking some, but you're supposed to talk to a doctor first before you do it, and I don't know who to ask."

Tommy put his pen down and squinted at me like I

was a moron. "Why don't you ask Dr. Young? I thought you went over there all the time. He probably has Band-Aids too, you know."

"Yeah, but . . ." I turned the Band-Aid box on its side. I couldn't go over to Rebecca's house to talk to her dad about vitamins if she was busy hating me. "You don't know any other doctors?"

He pointed to the Band-Aid box. "Put those back, okay?" Then he went back to his video game.

I slid the Band-Aids off the counter. "You should be nicer to me, you know," I told him as I put the box back on the shelf. "I have Ebola."

"No you don't," Tommy said, his game still beeping.

"I could," I said. "And then wouldn't you feel bad?"

He didn't answer, so I headed for the door.

All of a sudden the beeps stopped. "Hey, Annie?" Tommy called.

I turned around. "Yeah?"

"I'm having my birthday party on Friday," he said. "Bowling. It's just gonna be me and my parents, but my dad thought maybe you'd want to come too." He shrugged. "You know, 'cause you won't get to go this year with Jared. He thought you might want to come."

I thought about that.

"Friday?" I asked.

Tommy nodded. "Yeah. Six o'clock."

I ran my foot over a smudge on the floor. "Okay," I said after a while. "Sure. I mean, unless I can't. Because of the Ebola."

"Right." Tommy turned his video game back on. "See you then."

"See you."

When I got home, I decided to call Rebecca's house to make up with her. Then I could ask her dad about vitamins and get some Band-Aids, plus she'd be my friend again.

Tracey picked up the phone. "Young residence," she said, sounding sweet as peaches.

"Um, hi," I said. "Is Rebecca there?"

"Who's calling?"

"It's Annie. But tell her it's Grace Foley from school, 'kay?"

"Whatever." Tracy didn't tell Rebecca who it was at all, so I don't even know why she asked. She just hollered, "Rebecca! Phone!"

"Hello?" Rebecca said when she picked up the other line.

"Hi, it's me. Don't hang up."

"What do you want?" she asked.

That's when I realized that making up with someone who was still mad at you was harder than putting together a thousand-piece jigsaw puzzle with a blindfold on. I knew I had to think of just the perfect thing to say so she'd like me again. Too bad all I could think of was "How come you were hanging out with Doug yesterday at the picnic? You told me once he smells like boiled broccoli, and you hate broccoli."

Rebecca huffed out a giant puff of air. "Who else was I supposed to hang out with?" she said. "You're not my friend anymore."

I got an Ebola-feeling lurch in my stomach right then. "I'm not?" I said.

"No." And she hung up the phone.

sixteen
● ● ●

Lunch was SpaghettiOs from a can. I chewed
extra slow, making sure every bite was just mush before
I swallowed it down, so I wouldn't choke. Dad stared at
his spoon the whole time he was eating, except when
the spoon was in his mouth, when he stared at the
air. He didn't call me Moonbeam. He didn't call me
anything.

After Dad went back to his office, I decided I'd better fix my will since it had all people in it who I didn't
much want to leave stuff to anymore. But I couldn't
remember where I'd put it. I found a yellow pad of

paper and a pen on the coffee table in the living room, and I went out to the porch to write a new one.

Fifteen minutes later I was still sitting there, yellow paper staring at me blank, when from across the street I heard "Hello, Annie Z.!"

I looked up and there was Mrs. Finch, walking out her front door with a metal bucket full of stuff I couldn't see. I waved at her.

"What are you doing with that bucket?" I called over.

She tilted it so I could see inside. "My new gardening tools," she told me. "Care to help me do some weeding? This yard is a wreck."

I shrugged. "Okay," I said. "But let me go change first."

I picked up my pad of paper and went upstairs to change into long sleeves and pants. That's because weeding meant flowers, and flowers meant bees, and I knew from the book that bees usually only stung you on bare skin, so it was best to be as covered up as possible. When I was done changing, I pulled my hair through the back of a baseball cap I found in the laundry room and went back outside.

"Aren't you going to be hot in that?" Mrs. Finch said when I reached her lawn.

"I don't want to get bee stings," I told her. "I've never had one, so I could be deathly allergic—I don't know."

"I suppose that makes sense," she said with a tiny nod. I noticed she wasn't wearing her old-lady slacks like usual. Instead she had on khaki-colored overalls, with a bib and everything.

"So"—I plopped myself down next to her in front of her flower bed—"how do you weed?"

She handed me a tiny shovel thing and showed me how to dig up the plants so I got all the root parts. After a while I started to get really sweaty, and I figured since I hadn't seen a single bee so far, it would probably be safe to roll up my sleeves at least, so I did.

After a bit more digging, Mrs. Finch said to me, "So have you been reading that book I lent you?"

"Mmm-hmm," I said, as I plonked my shovel down deep into the dirt. "I've been reading a lot. They just brought Wilbur to the fair."

"Annie Z., I'm impressed!" Mrs. Finch tossed a weed into the garbage bag between us. "You're almost to the end. Are you liking it so far?"

"It's all right," I said, tugging at a plant that didn't want to be unstuck from the ground.

"Well, keep reading, okay? I know you'll like it."

We dug up weeds for a long time, until we were both smeared all over dirty. Mrs. Finch asked me all sorts of questions about the neighborhood, like who lived where and who was friendly and where my school was and what grocery store sold the freshest fruit and every sort of question like that. And we'd been digging and tugging and pulling for about an hour I guess, and there were still loads of weeds left, but all of a sudden Mrs. Finch yanked her hands out of the dirt and said, "These old fingers of mine are getting sore. What do you say we take a break?"

I wiped my hands on my pants and made two big dirt handprints. "Okay," I said.

"Great." She started to get to her feet creaky slow.

"How about I make us a pot of tea?"

I reached out a hand to Mrs. Finch to help her, because I was already standing and she still had one leg to go. "The same kind of tea as you gave me last time?" I asked as I pulled her up. "For my arm scrape, I mean?"

She stood up all the way, leaning on me. "I can make that one again, if you'd like."

"Well . . ." I thought about it. "I mean, it tasted good and everything. But do you have any . . . do you have any tea for Ebola?"

"Ebola?"

"Yeah," I said. "I think I might have it." Because even though my head didn't hurt much anymore and my stomachache was a little bit better too, Ebola wasn't something that went away. I figured the real bad symptoms were going to kick in any minute.

Mrs. Finch scratched at her nose. "Ebola tea?" she asked me.

"Uh-huh."

"I'll see what I can do, Annie Z." And we went inside.

I was surprised when I saw the living room, because almost all the boxes were gone already and everything practically was put away—books on the bookshelves, rugs on the floor. When Rebecca moved to our neighborhood, her family had boxes sitting around for weeks, with stuff spewing out the tops and onto the carpet. "Wow," I told Mrs. Finch. "You're a quick unpacker."

She laughed. "I guess I don't have much else to do with myself," she said.

There was still one box left, and it hadn't been opened at all—the tape was still stuck to the top tight. It was the box on the table by the fireplace, the one that said FRAGILE! And even though I kind of knew Mrs. Finch didn't want to talk about it, I pointed to it anyway. "You want help unpacking that one?" I asked.

Mrs. Finch just said, "Let's put the water on, shall we?" and walked into the kitchen. Which I could tell meant we were done talking about the box, but it sure didn't make me stop being curious.

While Mrs. Finch was putting water in the pot, I sat down at the kitchen table and asked, "Mrs. Finch?

Do your fingers get sore because you have arthritis?"

"As a matter of fact, I do," she said, turning off the faucet. "Rheumatoid arthritis. I've had it for years."

I nodded. "I read about that one," I told her. "You're supposed to drink lots of water. And eat pineapple, too. I don't know why. But the book said that helped."

"Huh." Mrs. Finch smiled at me as she set the pot on the stove. "I didn't know about the pineapple. I'll have to try that. Thanks, Annie Z."

"Sure."

While we were waiting for the water to get hot, Mrs. Finch got out a deck of cards so we could play go fish. We played four games and I won three. Then, when Mrs. Finch was pouring me another cup of Ebola tea, she said, "Time for a new game. I'm going to teach you how to play gin rummy."

"Gin rummy? What's that?"

"It's very fun. I think you'll like it. Here, hand me the deck. I'll shuffle."

Mrs. Finch showed me how to play gin rummy, and she was right—it was fun. She even showed me how to do betting. We bet a penny for every point, only they were imaginary pennies that Mrs. Finch wrote down on a pad of paper, because I was just a kid.

"Next time I come over, I'm gonna bring a bag of gummy bears," I told Mrs. Finch as I swiped up her three of diamonds from the table. "Then we can bet for those. And we can call it gummy rummy."

"Gummy rummy." Mrs. Finch laughed. "I like that."

It was funny, I thought, that here I was sitting playing cards in the haunted house, when just the week before I'd been trying to peek in the windows. I put down an ace. "You want to hear something, Mrs. Finch?"

"Absolutely," she said, and she looked at her cards with her eyes squinched together close, trying to fig- ure out which one to get rid of, I guess.

"My friend Rebecca thinks your house is haunted."

She plopped a seven into the pile. "She does?"

"Yeah," I said, fanning out my cards to look at them better. "She thinks there's ghosts and everything. Rebecca's crazy about ghosts. She's wanted to come inside here ever since the Krazinskys moved out."

"Well, why don't you invite her over then? I love having company."

I scooped up a card from the pile and tucked it into my hand. "I don't think she'd come if I asked her."

"Why's that?"

"Because I think she hates me."

"Now why on earth would she hate you?"

I picked the jack of diamonds out of my hand, because that was the card I wanted to get rid of. But I didn't set it down right away. I just sort of stared at it.

"Mrs. Finch?" I said after a little while staring. "Hamsters are different than brothers, right?"

She took a sip of her tea and then put her teacup back with a quiet clank in the saucer. "I don't think I understand the question, Annie Z."

"It's just . . . I mean, hamsters are pets, right? And when they die it's sad and maybe you have a funeral and you miss them and everything. And I *know* that. But when brothers . . ." I took another long gulp of tea. "When brothers die . . ." I swirled the last of the tea around the bottom of my cup.

"Annie?"

I looked up at Mrs. Finch then. "Jared died," I told her. "My brother Jared. He died."

"Oh, honey." She reached across the table and set her hand on top of mine, nice and warm. She looked me square in the eyeballs. "I already knew," she told me. "Mrs. Harper told me when I moved in. I should have said something earlier, I guess. But I thought you might not want to talk about it. I'm sorry."

"You knew?" I asked her.

She nodded.

"But then how come you never gave me the dead-brother look?"

"Annie Z.," Mrs. Finch said after another while of quiet, "I think I'd like to show you something."

"What?"

"It's in the living room. Why don't we refill our cups first?"

So Mrs. Finch poured us both more Ebola tea, and we left our cards facedown on the table, and we went into the living room with our teacups.

"Well," Mrs. Finch said when we got there, "would you like to open it, or should I?"

She was pointing to the box by the fireplace.

seventeen
●●●

I didn't know what was going to be in that box. Something FRAGILE!, that's all I knew for sure. Maybe it would be a whole bunch of porcelain dolls like the ones Mrs. Harper collected in a big glass case. Only I sort of hoped not, because their eyes were kind of creepy, and anyway what was the point of dolls you couldn't play with?

Mrs. Finch found some scissors in a drawer, and she handed them to me to cut the tape with. "You can set your tea on the floor," she said. "Right there, that's it."

I took an itty-bitty sip of Ebola tea and put my cup

on the floor, like Mrs. Finch said, and I cut a big slit in the tape. Then I pried open the two sides of the lid.

"Careful now," Mrs. Finch said. "Careful." She put her head right next to mine, and together we peeked inside.

It wasn't creepy porcelain dolls inside the box. I wasn't sure what it was, actually. All I could see was newspapers.

"What is it?" I asked Mrs. Finch.

She didn't answer, just took out one of the newspaper-wrapped things on top. It was long and flat in the shape of a rectangle, about the size of my big green book. She unwrapped it slowly and held it up so I could see.

It was a photograph of fish. A photo of a fish stuck in a frame. The fish was orange with thick white stripes outlined in black, and it was way up close, so you could see its fishy fins and all its fishy scales, and the water behind it was bright swimming-pool blue.

"Isn't it beautiful?" she asked me.

"Um," I said, "sure."

I guess it was kind of neat, if you liked fish. But I didn't think it was exactly the sort of thing I'd call "beautiful."

Mrs. Finch was unwrapping another thing, about the same size as the orange fish photo, so I figured it was probably another picture in a frame. I thought maybe it would be of a giraffe or a polar bear or something cool like that, but when she showed it to me, it was another fish. Lime green with yellow zigzags. She took out three more photos and unwrapped them and lined them up one by one on top of the box. She did it real careful, like they were babies.

And every single one of them was of fish.

"They're tropical," Mrs. Finch said, looking down at them and smiling. "Gorgeous, aren't they? This one's a clown fish, and this one's an angelfish, and this one's a golden neon goby."

"Mmm," I said.

I peeked inside the box while Mrs. Finch was busy getting google-eyed over her clown fish photo. There must've been thirty of them in there.

"My husband took them," she said.

I looked over at her face right then, and it was real sad, the saddest I'd ever seen her.

"What was his name?" I asked her.

"Nathan. He died about a year ago."

I nodded, slow up and down. "Did it happen all of a sudden?"

"No," she said. "He was very sick for a long time. He had cancer."

"Jared died all of a sudden," I told her. "There was a problem with his heart."

We just stood there for a while, the two of us, looking at those fish photos. But then Mrs. Finch grabbed a piece of newspaper and started wrapping it around the clown fish photo and placed it back in the box. Then she wrapped up the other ones too.

"You should put them up on the walls," I said. "They're really"—I tried to remember a good word from Dr. Young's word wall—"*stupefying*. You have lots of good places to put them."

She put the last photo in the box and then smoothed

the lid closed. "Oh, I don't know." She picked her tea-cup off the floor and took a long drink. "Maybe," she said, looking at me thoughtful. "Yes, maybe one day." She nodded then, like she really meant it. "But I'm not quite sure I'm ready yet." She took another sip. "Would you like to finish that game of cards now?"

So we went back to the kitchen and Mrs. Finch put on another pot of water for tea. I picked up my cards and looked at them, remembering what they all were. "Whose turn was it?" I asked.

"Yours, I think. To discard."

"Oh yeah." I set down my jack of diamonds. "What was your husband like?" I asked Mrs. Finch. "Nathan."

She picked up the jack and put it in her own hand. "He was very short," she said. "And he told terrible jokes. But he was incredibly smart. He was a scientist."

"Did he study lightning like Ben Franklin?" I asked. "We learned about Ben Franklin last year in school."

"He studied fish."

"Oh." I guess that made sense.

"What was Jared like?"

"He was . . ." I thought about it. It was hard to think up a way to talk about a person, when all you had was words to say it. "He was nice. He was the best brother ever."

Mrs. Finch smiled. "What sorts of things did he like to do?" she asked me, putting down a three of clubs.

"He liked to hang out with Tommy Lippowitz and play tackle baseball. Sometimes tackle dominoes." Mrs. Finch laughed. "Oh, and also"—I sat up straighter so I could tell the next part really good—"we used to play this one game all the time. Jared invented it. It's called the burrito game."

"The burrito game?"

"Uh-huh." I picked up a queen and got rid of a two. "The way you play is you put a blanket on the floor and you lie down on one side and hold on tight to the blanket and then roll over until you're wrapped up so hard you can barely breathe. The blanket is the tortilla and you're the beany filling. Then you have to stand up, which is the hard part, because burritos can't bend their knees, but after you're both standing, you get to dance around and sing the burrito song that Jared made up. It goes like

●●●

this: 'Isn't it neat-o to be a giant, giant burrito?'" I sang it the best I could, and Mrs. Finch laughed so hard, I thought maybe she'd drop all her cards, but I kept going because I wasn't done yet. "And when you get sick of singing, you bump your burrito stomachs together for a while like burrito sumo wrestlers, and after that you unroll yourself and eat chocolate pudding."

"Why chocolate pudding?" Mrs. Finch asked.

"'Cause it tastes good." I stared at my cards for a minute, but I wasn't really looking at them. Suddenly all sorts of thoughts about Jared were swirling around my brain, thoughts about the burrito game and bowling and his locked-up bedroom. "His birthday's this Sunday, you know," I said after a while.

"Oh, honey."

I set my cards facedown on the table and tilted my teacup a bit even though there wasn't tea in it anymore. "Mrs. Finch? Do you think . . . well, what do you think you're supposed to do on someone's birthday? If they're not around anymore, I mean. 'Cause, well, you can't have a birthday party, but it still *is* their birthday, right?"

She thought about that, tapping her cards on the edge of the table. "Maybe the best thing to do for Jared is simply to remember him," she said.

"But I remember Jared all the time," I told her. "And that doesn't feel like enough."

"Well . . ." Mrs. Finch kept on tapping her cards. "There are all sorts of ways to remember someone. For instance"—she plucked a card from the draw pile and slid it in between the ones in her hand—"Nathan and I lived in Sicily for a time. That's in Italy, in the south. There are several remarkable species of fish there." I nodded like I already knew that before, even though I didn't. Mrs. Finch put a four of spades down in the discard pile. "Anyway, in Italy, when someone dies, that person's family and friends write up a sort of story about him—all the nice things he did, and how great he was, and how much everyone loved him."

"Like a what-do-you-call-it," I said, picking up my cards again. "In the newspaper sometimes."

"An obituary." Mrs. Finch nodded. "Yes, it's very similar to that. But in this case they don't put the story in the newspaper. They print up dozens of copies, as large as movie posters sometimes, with the person's photo right at the top. And they plaster them all over the city—near churches, on storefronts, even on telephone poles. They stay up for weeks. So no matter where you go, you can remember the person and think nice things about him."

I picked up the four of spades and studied it. I wasn't sure about putting up movie posters all over town with Jared's face on them, but it was a start of an idea anyway. "You think I can come up with something good like that for Jared?"

"There's not a doubt in my mind, Annie Z.," she said, and she got up from the table. "How about another cup of tea? I think the water's ready."

"Thanks," I said, and she started pinching leaves out of her jars. "If I really do have Ebola, I'm gonna have to come over here all the time for more tea."

Mrs. Finch plunked the metal infuser into the cherry teapot and then came back to the table and sat down. She put two fingers on top of her pile of cards, but she didn't pick them up—she just sat there. Then finally she turned her eyes to me and said, "Annie, I think it's time for you to close your umbrella."

When she said that, I turned around and looked behind me, because I thought maybe there was someone else in her house named Annie who was holding an umbrella. Either that or she was bonkers. Because I definitely didn't have an umbrella. It wasn't even raining.

"Um, what?" I said, turning back around.

"Here's what I think," she told me, and she said it in a way that made me think she wasn't nutso, but I still wasn't one hundred percent sure about that. "When it's raining, you put up an umbrella, right? So you won't get wet?"

I shrugged a shoulder. "Guess so."

"But say you're out walking for a long time, holding your umbrella high up in the air to protect you against the rain. If you're too busy worrying about not getting wet, or just thinking about something else entirely, you may not even notice that it's stopped raining. So there you are, with your umbrella still open above you, and there's no more rain at all. You may not be getting wet, but you're missing the sunshine." She put her hands on the table, palms up, like she was about to say something really important. "Annie Z., I think all your worries are like an umbrella for you."

"Okay," I said slowly. "Except for that doesn't make any sense."

She smiled. "Well, if you spend all your time worrying," she said, "and thinking about helmets and Band-Aids and Ebola and gangrene and bee stings, then you won't have time to think about Jared, will you?" She gave me a look like she was checking to see if that was right, and I didn't nod or anything but I guess she could tell I thought maybe that sort of made sense just a little bit, because she went on talking. "It's easier to be worried than to be sad. At least I think it is. So you use worrying as a sort of protection."

I took in a deep breath and thought about it. I wasn't sure she was right, but I wasn't sure she was wrong either.

"Maybe," I said.

She nodded slowly, thinking some more, I guess.

"Well," she said after a few seconds, "that's just the thing. You don't need that protection anymore. Because the sun is starting to shine again. It's coming out slowly, but it's coming. And if you keep up your umbrella, then you're not ever going to see it."

I blinked one eye at Mrs. Finch, the right one, and I kept it closed, because that was the face I made when I was feeling *quizzical*. "Well, so," I said, and I said it real slow because I was still thinking out the words at the same time as I said them, "so how do I stop worrying?"

Mrs. Finch picked up her cards finally and looked at them. She switched two of them in her hand. "Perhaps it's time to stop reading that medical book of yours," she said, putting a king down in the pile.

I scooped it up. "My book? But I just got it back."

She shrugged. "How about this, Annie? If you promise to stop reading it, then as a treat I'll pick up some chocolate chips at the store and you can come over tomorrow afternoon to help me bake cookies. I've been meaning to try out my new oven."

"Aren't cookies bad for your cholesterol?"

Mrs. Finch raised her eyebrows at me.

"*Fine*," I said. "I'll stop reading the book."

"Excellent."

"But only if you put up your fish pictures."

She squinched her mouth over to one side. "Nathan's photos?" she asked.

"That's your umbrella," I told her.

She sighed, one hand around her empty teacup. "Oh, Annie, I don't know. . . ."

"I'll stop reading my book if you put up a fish picture. Just one."

She closed her right eye and looked at me for a while. I guess she was feeling *quizzical* too. "All right," she said at last. "I'll do it."

"Good. Let's go pick the photo. It better be a big one."

She laughed. "Okay, Annie Z."

"And you know what else?" I said.

"What's that?"

I put down a card in the pile, facedown, and smiled at her real big. "Gin," I told her.

eighteen

●●●

We put the fish photo up at one end of the living room, so you didn't see it right when you walked inside but you could still get a nice good look if you knew it was there. Mrs. Finch let me pick what one to put up, and I chose the big bright clown fish one because I liked his stripes.

Mrs. Finch smiled when I picked that one. "That was Nathan's favorite too," she said.

I hammered in the nail at just the right spot. Mrs. Finch let me do it by myself because I told her my dad let me use his hammer all the time. That was sort of a lie, but I didn't hurt my thumb or anything. When the picture was up, we walked to the other side of the room to make sure it wasn't crooked.

"You know, Annie Z.," Mrs. Finch said, putting a hand on my shoulder, "that looks pretty nice. I'm glad you made me hang it up."

"You think you'll ever put up the rest of them?" I asked her.

"Maybe one day I will. But for now one seems like enough."

And I thought that made some sense.

"You feel your umbrella closing yet?" I said.

She thought about it. "Maybe just a smidgen."

After that I went home, but I told Mrs. Finch I'd come back at two o'clock tomorrow for cookies. The whole way home I thought about how I could just keep reading that green book if I wanted, and not do my part of the deal. Mrs. Finch would probably never know, and then I could look up more diseases. But then when I got upstairs, I saw Jared's door across the hallway, closed tight as always, and I figured if I really did have an umbrella like Mrs. Finch said, well, I might as well try to close it.

I found the big green book where I'd hidden it in my shorts drawer, and I got out a clean piece of stationery—the kind with the kittens on it that Rebecca had given me for Christmas—and I sat down on my bed to write a letter.

Dear Mrs. Harper,

Here is your book back, which you didn't know I took but I did. I'm sorry. That was not a nice thing for a Junior Sunbird to do. And I'm sorry about the lying. And for the hosing. Those weren't nice Junior Sunbird things either. I think maybe I'm not a very good one.

Sorry.

~~Your friend,~~

~~Sincerely,~~

Your friend,

Annie Richards

Then I tucked the letter inside the big green book so that just the *Dear Mrs. Harper* part was sticking out the top. And I walked next door and put the whole thing inside the Harpers' mailbox. It just barely fit.

After I closed the mailbox door, I stood on Mrs. Harper's lawn for a second with my eyes closed, trying to feel if maybe I had an imaginary umbrella that had gone closed a little bit. But I couldn't tell for sure. Then I tried to feel if I had real Ebola, but I couldn't tell that either.

Right about dinnertime the phone rang and I answered it.

"Hello?"

"Hey, sweetie." It was Mom. "How are you doing?"

I shrugged, even though you weren't supposed to shrug over the phone. Mom usually got mad when I did that, but this time she didn't say anything.

"I just wanted to let you know that I have to stay at work late tonight. I probably won't be home until after you're asleep."

"Okay," I said.

"You'll tell your dad?"

"Sure."

"Thanks. And sweetie?"

I tucked up the edge of my arm-scrape Band-Aid to see how my scab was coming. Still pretty scabby. "Mmm-hmm?"

"I love you, you know."

There was a pause after that, but I didn't say anything. I couldn't think of anything I wanted to say. But just when I could tell Mom was getting ready to hang up the phone, I thought of something.

"Hey, Mom?"

"Yes, sweetie?"

"Can you take me to get a present for Tommy's birthday on Friday? He invited me bowling."

She didn't answer.

"Mom? You still there?"

"You know, Annie," she said after another second of waiting, "I just don't think I'm going to get a chance to do that before Friday. Why don't you make him a nice card or something?"

"But I think he wants walkie-talkies," I said. My forehead felt hot. I put my hand up to feel if I had a fever from the Ebola, but I couldn't tell.

"We can talk about it tomorrow, all right?"

"Fine."

"Night, sweetie."

"Night."

For dinner we had pizza. Dad ordered olives and pepperoni, even though I hated olives. I told him that, and he said he forgot, which didn't really surprise me much.

"Dad?" I asked, when there was mostly only crusts left in the box.

"Mmm?" he said, still chewing. He was reading a magazine while we ate, which Mom always said was not good table manners.

"Can you take my temperature?" I asked, picking the last four olives off my slice of pizza. "I think I have Ebola."

Dad just nodded, so I ran upstairs to get the thermometer from the medicine cabinet, and when I got back, Dad placed it under my tongue, just the way Dr. Young did.

"I'll be right back to check," he said.

But when the thermometer beeped a minute later, Dad wasn't back yet. I kept it under my tongue for five whole minutes, watching the clock over the stove. Finally I took it out and checked it myself.

Ninety-eight-point-six. Exactly normal.

I found Dad in the living room watching TV.

"Dad," I said from the doorway. My voice was pointy little icicles.

"What?"

I waved the thermometer at him. "You were supposed to come back and check my temperature," I told him.

"Oh," he said. "Sorry."

I just rolled my eyes and headed back upstairs, careful to wipe off the thermometer with rubbing alcohol before I put it back in its case in the medicine cabinet. If I got swept away in an avalanche that second, Dad would probably forget to care.

nineteen

●●●

The next afternoon Mrs. Finch opened her front door with a big smile.

"Right on time!" she greeted me. One of the buttons was open on her ugly blue grandma sweater, and I could see her stripy blue-and-green blouse peeking out from underneath, but I didn't tell her. I sort of didn't want her to fix it. I liked her that way, one button off. "Did you keep your part of the bargain? Are you ready for cookie baking?"

"Yep," I said with a nod. "I'm ready." Ever since I'd written that letter to Mrs. Harper telling her I'd stolen her book, I kept waiting for her to yell at me about it. Probably she'd storm over to my house angry as a scorpion and tell me I was out of the troop for good, and make me hand over my outfit and my three measly badges too. But that hadn't happened yet. Maybe she was out of town.

"Well, come on in," Mrs. Finch said.

She led me through the house to the kitchen. But when I got there, I froze still as a statue. Because Mrs. Finch wasn't the only person in her house.

"I don't think there are any ghosts in here, Mrs. Finch." It was Rebecca, and she was closing the lid on the fish-shaped cookie jar. "It's probably safe to put cookies in there." Then she looked up and saw me. "Oh," she said. And just the way she said it, I could tell she hadn't been expecting me either.

Mrs. Finch looked at me and then looked at Rebecca. "Yes, I suppose I should explain, shouldn't I?" She bent down and started rummaging around in a bottom cupboard. "You see, I just happened to be talking to Rebecca's mother on the phone yesterday, and

I remembered that Rebecca was a big fan of haunted houses. And as you know, my house may very well be haunted. Aha!" she cried, pulling out two baking sheets. She stood up. "So I thought she might like to come over and bake cookies in one. I suppose I forgot to mention that you would also be here, Annie Z. I do apologize to both of you."

I rolled my eyes at her. It was a good thing Mrs. Finch wasn't a professional spy, because she was a terrible liar.

"Now that we've cleared that up"—she clapped her hands together like we were having a sleepover party—"let's get baking, shall we?"

Rebecca was chewing hard on one of her braids, and I would've bet ten whole dollars she was trying to decide which was worse, baking cookies with me or leaving the haunted house once she finally got in it.

She stayed.

"Okay," Mrs. Finch said, handing Rebecca the bag of chocolate chips. "Rebecca, why don't you read the ingredients, and Annie, you can make sure we have everything we need. I'll get out the mixing bowls."

Rebecca did an eyeball glare at me for a full twenty seconds, but then she started to read off the back of the bag. "Flour," she said. She sounded like she was reading the ingredients for rat poison.

I sighed and monkeyed up onto Mrs. Finch's counter to dig through her top cupboard. I wondered if Rebecca would ever stop hating me.

"Careful now, Annie Z!" Mrs. Finch cried just as I located the flour.

"Sugar," Rebecca read.

"Brown or normal?" I asked.

I could tell she didn't want to answer me, but probably she figured that if she didn't tell me the right kind of sugar, the cookies wouldn't taste good. "Um . . . both," she said.

When we found all the ingredients, we started mixing everything up in bowls. I let Rebecca break the eggs, even though that was my second favorite part, because I knew she liked doing it too. I caught her glancing at me sideways when she was cracking the last egg into the bowl, but when I tried to smile at her, she looked away real quick.

"So, Rebecca," Mrs. Finch said while Rebecca started dumping the flour mixture into the bowl with the eggs. I stood there pretending I was helping. "How long have you been a paranormal enthusiast?"

"Huh?" Rebecca said. Which was exactly what I was thinking.

"How long have you been interested in ghosts?"

"Oh." Rebecca whacked the bowl with a spoon to get out the last of the flour. "I dunno. A long time, I guess."

"Personally," Mrs. Finch went on, "I'm not sure I believe in any of that, but I suppose you never know. Which are the most interesting to you, ghosts or poltergeists?"

Mrs. Finch was doing a good job trying, but I could tell that Rebecca was busy figuring out in her brain how long cookies took to bake so she could go home. She was staring at her spoon real hard. "I don't know," she said slowly. "They're both good, I guess. I think we add the chocolate chips now, right?"

While I was wrestling the bag of chocolate chips

open, I tried to shoot Mrs. Finch a just-give-up-now look, but she ignored me.

"So then, Rebecca, what are your hobbies?"

Rebecca didn't answer for a while, just watched as I poured in the chips. Probably it was only a couple seconds, but I couldn't stand the quiet anymore.

"She does ballet!" I said. It came out a little louder than I wanted.

"Well, that's lovely."

"And piano playing too!" For some reason I couldn't stop being loud. Rebecca's face was turning red as she watched me pour the chips into the cookie dough, so I tried to make my voice more quiet. "She's a real good piano player," I told Mrs. Finch.

Mrs. Finch nodded at me but didn't say anything.

I sighed.

Mrs. Finch was stirring the dough up with a wooden spoon, but it was too thick and the chips weren't mixing in. "Looks like we'll have to go in with our hands," she said. "Anyone feel like getting a little messy?"

I almost said I'd do it, because that was my number-

192

one favorite part of baking cookies, when the dough got up in the in-between parts of your fingers and you couldn't even get it out with washing—there was only one way to clean it up, and that was licking. But I decided better and didn't say anything so Rebecca could do it instead.

But she didn't say anything either.

"Really?" Mrs. Finch said. "Neither of you wants to do it? I always thought that was the best part when I was a youngster." She looked at both of us, but we only stood there, silent as weeds. "All right then," she said, rolling up her sleeves. "I guess I'll have to go in myself."

"Wait!" Rebecca hollered, just as Mrs. Finch had the tippy tip of her pointer finger aimed for the dough. I figured she finally came to her senses and was going to volunteer. But I was wrong. "Annie should do it," she said.

Mrs. Finch still had her hands stuck like frozen fish sticks over the bowl. "Oh?" she said. She looked at me, but I didn't say anything.

"Yeah," Rebecca told her, and she said it soft. "That's her favorite part."

Mrs. Finch smiled at me and wiped her hands on her apron, even though they weren't dirty. "Well then," she said, and she scooched the bowl across the counter in my direction, "I suppose Annie should be the one to do it."

I looked at her, my hands tight around both sides of the bowl, and then I looked at Rebecca. And even though she blinked real quick and looked down the instant her eyeballs met mine, I thought she didn't look quite so mad as before.

"Thanks," I said. I stuck my hands deep in the cookie dough and felt the squishy way it oozed between my fingers.

While the cookies were in the oven baking, I asked Mrs. Finch if I could take Rebecca on a tour of the house. "Just to see if any of the haunted things are still left," I said.

"Sure thing," Mrs. Finch said, setting the timer on the oven. "Feel free to snoop around wherever you like. Oh, and be sure to check the hall closet, will you? The door squeaks horribly. It's probably an enraged spirit."

So I showed Rebecca all over the house. She was more excited than a mouse in a cheese factory. She peeked her nose between the coats in the hall closet, stuck her head under the bed, even lifted up the toilet seat in the bathroom.

"What are you looking for in there?" I asked her, sitting on the edge of the bathtub.

Rebecca shrugged. "I dunno. Maybe water ghosts. They like to haunt the pipes, you know."

"Oh." I thought about that for a second and then turned on the tub faucet to check in there. I couldn't see anything that didn't look like water. I turned it off. "Rebecca?"

"Yeah?" She was looking inside the medicine cabinet.

"I'm sorry about Fuzzby."

She stuck her braid in her mouth and chewed, still peeking into the medicine cabinet. "It's okay," she said after a while, plopping her braid out. She didn't look at me, though. "You were right. He was just a hamster. It wasn't like when Jared died. I shouldn't have got so mad at you."

"But I liked him," I said. "Really. You still want to have a funeral for him? I'll help you, I promise." I didn't really want to do that, but I figured sometimes friends had to do things they didn't want to, especially if they'd said mean things and maybe hosed the other friend too.

"My mom helped me," Rebecca said, lifting up a jar of face goop to peek underneath. "With the funeral, I mean. It was okay."

"Oh," I said.

"I'm getting a new hamster. Next week." And finally she looked over at me. "Want to help me pick it out?"

I didn't. Not really. I didn't want to pick out a new hamster for Rebecca when there was no new Jared for me. But it was different, I knew it was, and I could tell Rebecca knew it too. "Sure," I said. "I'll help."

"Cool."

When we got back to the kitchen, Mrs. Finch was just pulling the last batch of cookies out of the oven. "Well?" she asked us. "How's my house look? See any spirits?"

Rebecca shook her head, so her two blond braids whipped across her shoulders. "I didn't see anything," she said. "But I'm pretty sure I felt their presence."

While we were eating the cookies, Mrs. Finch and I taught Rebecca how to play gummy rummy, only without the gummy part. We played for about an hour until Rebecca's mom called and said it was time for Rebecca to go home. After Mrs. Finch packed her up with extra cookies, we walked Rebecca to the door while she strapped on her bike helmet. "Well!" she hollered at us. "I'm going home now!"

"Okay!" I said, shouting loud like I had a bike helmet on too. "I'll see you later!"

And Rebecca didn't say "maybe" or "I'll think about it" or "don't hold your breath." She said, "Yeah! Call me later!"

And she biked off down the street.

It wasn't until I got all the way back to my house that I realized something. I hadn't worried about Ebola or gangrene or *E. coli* or poison oak once all afternoon.

twenty

●●●

Dad dropped me off at the Bowling Barn Friday evening, and I was ten minutes late, but Tommy and his parents hadn't started bowling yet. Mrs. L. was picking out a bowling ball and Tommy was typing on the computer that kept track of the scores.

"Hey, Annie," he said when he saw me coming. He typed out some letters on the keyboard. "You ride your bike here?"

"What?" I said, because I thought that was a weird thing to ask. But then I remembered I was still wearing my bike helmet from the car, and I took it off quick and plopped it on one of the red plastic seats. "This is for you," I told him. I held out his present, which was the chocolate chip cookies I'd baked at Mrs. Finch's house stuffed into a Christmas tree tin I'd found in the hall closet. That was Rebecca's idea. She'd come over to my house that afternoon with a bag of gummy bears, and we'd spent almost the whole day playing gummy rummy.

Tommy opened the tin and took a bite of one of the cookies. "Thanks," he said. And then he went back to typing.

After that Mr. L. took me to get bowling shoes. I was size five, but even the size sevens weren't big enough to fit around my feet with my ankle bandages on.

"Can't you take those off?" the shoe guy asked me. His name tag said CHARLES.

"But they're for ankle sprains," I told him. "What if I twist wrong while I'm bowling and I have to go to the hospital and they end up amputating my foot off?"

He looked at Mr. L., who shrugged.

"I really don't think that's ever happened before,"

Charles said after a second.

I thought about it. "Can't I just wear my regular shoes?"

"Sorry," he said. "Bowling Barn rules."

"You don't have to play, Annie," Mr. L. said. "You can just watch, if that's what you want."

I sat there for a minute, with my regular shoe in my left hand and the bowling one in my right hand. From behind me I could hear bowling balls shuttling down the lanes and pins knocking over *crash!* Oldies music my parents liked was blaring out of the speakers, and people were laughing and talking, and lights were flashing green to red to blue.

I could call my dad, I figured, and have him pick me up and go home and not have any amputations to worry about ever.

Or I could bowl.

"Annie?" Mr. L. said again.

"I'll wear the shoes," I said, bending over to unwrap my ankle bandages.

By the fifth frame I was in second place to Tommy,

but I was pretty sure Tommy's parents were losing on purpose.

"You're up, Batgirl!" Mr. L. called when it was my turn to go. Tommy had given us all weird names on the screen, which he said were out of comic books. I didn't mind mine too much. At least I wasn't Major Disaster. That was Tommy's mom.

I picked up the neon pink bowling ball that Mrs. L. had helped me pick out. It was the lightest one they had—so even if I dropped it on my foot, it probably wouldn't bruise me too bad. It also had extra-big finger holes, so I wouldn't get pinched.

"Come on, Batgirl!" Mrs. L. hollered as I stepped up to the line.

"It's going to be a strike," Mr. L. told me. "I can feel it."

I pulled back the ball with my right hand, aimed just the way Mr. L. had showed me, and swung, making extra careful sure not to let it go too soon and accidentally whack someone. It thundered down the lane.

Strike!

Tommy's parents stood up and cheered, and the screen hanging from the ceiling flashed BATGIRL! BATGIRL! BATGIRL! Tommy gave me a thumbs-up.

"Hey, pretty good," he said when I sat down.

"Thanks," I said.

"Oh, by the way. I was supposed to give you this." He picked up a piece of paper from under the pile of sweaters on the seat next to him and handed it to me. The paper was bright yellow and folded in half, and scotch-taped at the edges like it was a top-secret document.

"What is it?" I asked.

He shrugged. "I dunno. Doug handed it to me at the store today and told me to give it to you."

"Doug Zimmerman?" I peeled off the tape with my fingernail and opened it.

It was a yellow flyer that used to say "Cheap Art Lessons with Louise!" but Doug had crossed out most of the words and written in new ones. Now it read "Free Obstacle Course Lessons with Doug!" And there was a picture on it that I think was supposed to be a

person limboing under a pool noodle, but Doug definitely needed to take Louise's art lessons, because it
looked more like a German shepherd getting hit over
the head with a giant pencil.

"That's weird," Tommy said, reading over my
shoulder.

"Yeah," I said. I put the flyer back underneath the
pile of sweaters.

"Wolverine!" Mr. L. called, pointing to Tommy. "It's
your turn."

Tommy won that game with ninety-six points, and I
came in second with seventy-two. For the second game,
Tommy named us all after pirates. I said no thank you
to the hot dog Mr. L. offered me, but I did eat half the
nachos, because those didn't have meat in them so I
figured I probably wouldn't get food poisoning.

While we were waiting for Charles to unstick Mrs.
L.'s ball from behind the pins, I shifted in my hard red
chair to look at Tommy. I couldn't stop thinking about
how today was his twelfth birthday. And how even
though Jared's twelfth birthday was coming up in just

●●●

two days, Jared would never be twelve.

I guess Tommy saw me staring at the side of his face, because he scrunched up his eyebrows and looked at me funny. "What?" he said.

I ran a finger along the seam of my shorts, just studying the stitches for a while. "I'm sorry you have to have your birthday with me," I said finally. "Instead of Jared. I know it's not as good."

Tommy let out a puff of air. Then he told me, "I've been thinking about what you said, you know."

"Huh?"

"What you were asking about before. About wills. What I'd give to people and all that?"

I clacked the heels of my bowling shoes on the floor and noticed a pencil rolling around by my left foot. "Oh, yeah," I said. I waited for Tommy to keep talking, but he didn't. "So?"

"Yeah," he said, nodding slow. "I was just thinking that I don't think I'd have one."

Down at the very end of the lane, I could see Charles's head bobbing behind the pins, still trying to get Mrs. L.'s ball. "How come?" I asked.

"Well, I guess if I had a million dollars or something I would." He picked up the cookie tin from the seat between us and took out another cookie. "But I just have stuff. And I think people don't need my stuff to remember me." He took a bite and held out the tin to me so I could take a cookie too. "I guess I think people will just remember me 'cause of things I did."

For someone who didn't talk much, Tommy sure had lots to say. I ate the rest of my cookie thoughtful slow. And then, after the last swallow, I bent down to snatch the pencil off the floor, and I pulled the yellow flyer out from the sweaters.

"What are you doing?" Tommy asked me.

"Writing down the things I remember about Jared," I said. I wrote "burrito game," on the back of the flyer, on the blank side.

Tommy nodded and pulled one leg underneath him. "Put down 'tackle baseball,'" he said.

"Ooh," I said, scribbling fast. "That's a good one."

Tommy and I thought up lots of things to remember

about Jared, dozens and dozens, and I wrote them all down.

"You know," I said, halfway through writing "Cheerio-eating contest," "I think Doug stole this off the bulletin board in front of your store." There was a pinhole at the top, right in the center.

Tommy just shrugged. "That one's been up forever. I bet the whole town's seen it fifty times already."

"Yeah," I said, and I went back to writing.

But that got me to thinking, with an itch in my brain that I just knew was the start of a good idea. The more things Tommy and I thought up to write down, the itchier my brain got, full of thoughts about Lippy's, and the posters Mrs. Finch had told me about in Italy, and what Tommy had said about remembering. And by the time we'd finished our second game of bowling, me and Tommy had come up with the perfect way to celebrate Jared's birthday.

twenty-one

●●●

About ten o'clock Saturday morning I strapped on all my gear and walked down to Lippy's. While Mr. L. was stocking the warmer full of chicken wings, Tommy and I worked on our plan for Jared's birthday the next day.

"So you'll type it up on your computer?" I asked him, smoothing out the piece of scratch paper we'd been writing our rough draft on.

"Yep," Tommy said. "I'll make it look real professional, I promise."

"Good."

After I huffed my way back up Maple Hill, I figured I'd spend the rest of the day playing gummy rummy at Rebecca's. But when I got to her house, her mom said she wasn't there.

"Really?" I asked, yanking on my helmet strap. It was awfully sweaty under the chin. "But I thought she'd be back from ballet by now."

"She went over to Doug's house," her mom said. "About twenty minutes ago."

"She did?" That was weird. Now that Rebecca was friends with me again, what did she need to hang out with stupid Doug Zimmerman for?

"Apparently they're working on a *top secret project*." Rebecca's mom laughed. "But I'm sure they wouldn't mind if you went over too."

"Oh," I said. I tugged at my helmet strap again. "Yeah. Well, maybe."

I decided not to go to Doug's. I didn't know why Rebecca was there, but if I went over, Doug would probably try to give me obstacle course lessons, whatever those were. And I definitely did not want to do any obstacle courses.

Instead I figured maybe I'd do some reading. But since I didn't have my big green book anymore, it had to be *Charlotte's Web*. I dug it out from the pillows on top of my bed, where I'd stuffed it after the fireworks. Six of the pages were bent halfway over, and page fifty-eight was ripped in the middle. I was hoping Mrs. Finch wouldn't be too mad about that. Dr. Young always said that books were for reading, and if people wanted to keep them pristine and beautiful, they would've put them in museums instead of libraries. Personally I thought that was a pretty good way to think about things, but I put a piece of Scotch tape over the rip just in case Mrs. Finch didn't agree. Then I plopped down on my bed to read the chapter called "Uncle."

It wasn't a bad book, really, if you liked books about pigs. Anyway, the part about the fair was interesting. Fern rode on the Ferris wheel with a boy, and Wilbur was hoping to win a big prize, and Templeton the rat went off to stuff himself full of carnival food.

But when Charlotte the spider said she was

"languishing," I closed the book with a snap. That word had been up on Dr. Young's word wall once, and I knew for a fact it wasn't a good one.

I was out my front door and halfway across the street before I realized I'd forgotten to put on my bike helmet. But I looked both ways and didn't see any cars coming, so I kept going, the book tucked close to my chest.

"Hello, Annie Z.," Mrs. Finch greeted me after I rang her doorbell six times all in a row. Then she got a good look at me and frowned. "Is everything okay? You look upset."

I held out the book to her. "Charlotte's sick," I said. "You didn't tell me that was going to happen."

"Oh, sweetie," Mrs. Finch said, her voice thick as cream. She took the book and then grabbed hold of my hand too. "Come on inside. I'll put the tea on."

Fifteen minutes later we were sitting on the back deck, on Mrs. Finch's brand-new wooden porch swing with the dark blue flowery cushions. Mrs. Finch rocked softly with her feet, tipping the swing back and forth, back and forth. I kicked off my sneakers and socks and tucked my legs up to my chest, and took a small sip of my heartache tea, fresh from the teapot. Mrs. Finch opened up the book where I'd told her.

I closed my eyes while she read, her words coming out like rainwater. Mrs. Finch was a good reader. When she got to the chapter called "Last Day," I took another deep swallow of tea, and I concentrated hard on the words Charlotte was telling Wilbur, about how one day, after the winter, everything would be nice and warm and sunny again.

"'The song sparrow will return and sing, the frogs will awake, the warm wind will blow again. . . .'"

But Mrs. Finch stopped reading after that, and I opened my eyes to find out why. She was gazing out at her backyard, still rocking the swing slowly back and forth. I could tell just by the look on her face, the look that wasn't-quite-happy-wasn't-quite-sad, that she was thinking all the same thoughts I'd been thinking about Jared. Only hers were about her husband.

I set my teacup down careful on the deck, and then

I leaned over in the swing and scooped the book out of Mrs. Finch's lap. She looked up at me, surprised, and I started to read, right where she'd left off.

"'All these sights and sounds and smells will be yours to enjoy, Wilbur—this lovely world, these precious days.'"

By the time we got to the last word on the last page, our cups of tea were empty and I had a lump in my throat that ached when I swallowed. But I was pretty sure it wasn't tonsillitis.

"That was a good book," I told Mrs. Finch.

"I'm glad you liked it, Annie Z.," she said.

"You know," I told her, rocking the swing slowly with my feet, "I think maybe my umbrella really is closing a little bit, like you said."

"Really?" Mrs. Finch asked.

"Yeah. Maybe just a smidgen."

● ● ●

twenty-two

● ● ●

That night I woke up all of a sudden, and I could tell from the mud-darkness outside that it was later than I'd ever been up before. At first I couldn't figure out what had woken me up like that, and I worried for a second that I might have a sleeping disorder. But then I heard a noise coming from outside my bedroom, which was sort of like the sound Mr. Normore's wiener dog made when he was sniffing out something tasty, and I figured that must've been what woke me up. So I stuffed my feet into my alligator slippers and went to investigate.

The sniffling was coming from Dad's office, where the door was partway open. I was a little bit afraid, but I peeked my head in anyway, just to get a look.

Mom was in there, wearing her bathrobe she always wore at bedtime, the fuzzy peach one with the satin trim. Just like normal. But what wasn't normal at all was that she was sitting down at my dad's desk, holding his wall calendar, and she was crying.

Then, while I watched from the doorway, she ripped the calendar right in half and threw the two pieces on the floor. Even from where I was standing, I could see the big red circle on the calendar around July 9, and the words *Jared's B-day!!!* in giant letters.

I put my hands in the pockets of my pajama pants. "You can't rip up all the calendars in the world, you know," I told her.

Mom looked up then. "Oh, Annie," she said. And she opened up her arms the way she used to when I was tiny and I'd crawl into her lap so she could read to me. And even though I was way too big to sit in her lap anymore, I did it anyway. She pulled me close and then she put her hand on my arm-scrape Band-Aid, patting it smooth a few times, like she was trying to make it all better with just her fingers. "I keep telling you you're fine, don't I?" she said, and she blinked out some more tears. "But the truth is none of us are. How could we be?"

I thought about that. Then I reached up to smudge away a tear that was tracing its way down her cheek. "We just need to close our umbrellas," I told her.

Mom blinked a couple times. "Umbrellas?"

And so I explained about closing up the imaginary umbrellas, and how for Mrs. Finch that meant putting up fish pictures, and for me it meant reading books about pigs instead of books about diseases.

"So what do you think my umbrella is?" Mom asked when I was done with the explaining. I was still sitting in her lap, and she was rocking me soft. She had a few sniffles left in her, but she was mostly done crying.

I didn't answer right away. Instead I stood up and grabbed Mom's arm and made her walk with me into the hallway.

She stopped cold when we got to Jared's door. "Oh, Annie," she said, and she shook her head. "I don't know. . . ."

But I was the one who knew all about umbrellas, and I wasn't going to let Mom get out of it. "We'll do it together," I told her. So Mom went to get the key, and when she came back, we reached out, our two hands together, and we turned it in the lock.

As soon as we opened the door, it was like Jared was standing there with us, because it smelled exactly like him—dirt on his sneakers and Tootsie Rolls and orange-scented hand soap from Tommy's house. I didn't even know Jared had a smell until right that very second.

"Come on," I whispered to Mom, and we inched inside.

Parts of the room looked exactly like before Jared died, with his baseball posters on the wall and his robot collection on the shelf and his Einstein mug on his dresser filled up with quarters. But other parts weren't Jared-like at all. The bed was made up nice, corners tucked in and everything, and his clothes were hung up neatly or folded away in his drawers, instead of spewing out all everywhere the way they usually were. And the floor was vacuumed, row after row of ruler-straight vacuum lines, not a speck in sight.

Mom took a deep breath and then walked across the room, her feet leaving Mom-sized footprints on the perfect floor. She sat down gentle on the bed and looked around her. She wasn't crying anymore.

"What do we do now?" she asked.

I crossed the room and sat down next to her.

"I dunno," I said with a shrug. "Just sit, I guess."

I never thought that'd be how I'd spend the night before my brother's twelfth birthday—up past midnight sitting in his room with my mom in her peach bathrobe. But actually, it was sort of okay. After a while Mom stood up and tugged open the middle drawer of Jared's dresser. Then she pulled out a blue-and-green striped T-shirt and held it close to her face.

She looked over at me. "We should take his things to the thrift store," she said. "His clothes at least."

217
● ● ●

"Yeah?" I said.

She nodded. "People could use them, I think." She buried her nose in Jared's shirt again.

"I think that's a real good idea, Mom."

"You do?"

"Mmm-hmm."

Mom looked around the room for a minute. "Why don't we organize tomorrow?" she said. "We'll pack up his clothes, and you can help me go through his toys and things, and let me know which ones you might like, or if there's anything we should give to Tommy, or one of his friends at school . . ."

I stood up then, and I hugged her. Right around the middle.

She laughed. "What was that for?"

"Nothing," I said.

She hugged me back. "I love you, too, Annie," she said.

So far the umbrella-down project had been working pretty well, it seemed like. But there was still one person I needed to work on.

"Mom?" I said. "Would you do me a favor?"

"Anything in the world."

I pulled out of her arms and looked her square in the face. "I need you to teach me to make coffee," I told her.

twenty-three

●●●

The instant I woke up Sunday morning, my brain reminded me it was Jared's birthday. I stretched my feet out so they were straining tippy-toe straight, and I reached my arms to the very edges of my bed, fingers pointed, to make sure I was feeling okay. And it turned out I was. No headache, no earache, no sore throat, no stomach troubles. So I got up, dug through my laundry hamper until I found my favorite outfit— my yellow tiger T-shirt and the shorts with the flower for a pocket—and I got dressed. Then I padded into the hallway.

It was still early morning, with the sunlight just thinking about edging its way into the sky, and as far as I could tell, I was the first person up. I tiptoed down the stairs and opened our front door to get the newspaper off the porch where the paper boy threw it every Sunday.

Just as I was scooping up the paper, I noticed a small white envelope propped up between two slats, about five inches from my foot.

I picked it up.

Miss Annie Richards

That's what it said on the envelope. I didn't know who it was from, but I figured it was all right to go ahead and open it, since it had my name on it.

There was a folded-up letter in there, and something else small and flat—I couldn't tell what it was. I went for the letter first.

Dear Annie,

Thank you for returning the book, and for your nice note. It meant a lot to me. I think you are a much better Sunbird than you know.

Your friend,
Joanne Harper

I poked my fingers inside the envelope and took out the flat thing, then laid it in my hand. It looked just like a Junior Sunbird badge, the same size as a lid on an olive jar, with stiff purple fabric and yellow thread all around the outside. Only it wasn't an official badge—I could tell Mrs. Harper had made it herself on her sewing machine, because the letters on the inside were a little bit more lopsided than normal, and they spelled out "Apology Badge."

I ran my thumb across it as I walked back inside with the newspaper.

Four whole badges.

Fifteen minutes later I was sitting at the table with

the newspaper folded up in front of me when Dad came down the stairs. He rubbed his eyes when he saw me.

I pushed his mug across the table toward him. It was filled up with coffee, fresh and steaming, just the way Mom had showed me how to make it the night before. I'd put in the perfect amount of milk that he liked, too, until it was the same color as the inside of an almond. "Good morning, Dad," I said. "Care to read with me?"

Dad blinked once. Then twice. Then he smiled a twitch of a smile and sat down in the chair next to me. "I'd love to," he said.

And that morning, for the first time since Jared died, Dad and I read the newspaper together, the whole thing. While we were starting up the crossword puzzle, Dad leaned over and squeezed me tight into a sideways hug. "I've missed this, Moonbeam," he said, his voice tissue-paper soft. "Thank you."

We stayed in that hug for a bit, and that plus the Moonbeam made me feel warm all over.

"Twenty-six across is 'llama,'" I told him.

After a while Mom came into the kitchen, and she smiled at us and said, "The coffee turned out okay, then?" I nodded. I could tell by the way her eyes were shiny-wet in the corners that her brain had reminded her about Jared's birthday too. But Dad poured her a cup of coffee and she sat at the table and helped us with the crossword and we ate breakfast together. When we were finished eating, I told Mom and Dad I had something to show them. Me and Tommy's surprise.

"At Lippy's," I said. "I think you'll like it."

When we got down to the store, sure enough, there was Tommy, putting up our flyer on the bulletin board just like he'd promised. He stuck it right in the center, with a thumbtack in each corner. It wasn't as big as a movie poster, just regular flyer size on plain white paper, but it had giant letters at the top that said "Happy Birthday, Jared!" so I knew lots of people would notice it. Tommy stepped back so we could all read it.

Happy Birthday, Jared!

from Annie Richards and Thomas Lippowitz

Jared Richards was a real good friend and a real good brother. Today, July 9, is his birthday.

Here are some ways to remember him:

1. Eat Jared's favorite kind of ice cream (chocolate chip with crumbled-up animal crackers)
2. Roller-skate down Maple Hill with one eye closed
3. Play the burrito game (Annie will teach you how if you don't already know it)
4. Go miniature golfing
5. Start a robot war
6. Make turkey meat loaf and add loads of ketchup

Then we'd left lots of blank lines under that, so other people could add their own ideas. Dad scratched his head for a bit while he read our list, and then he picked up the pen that Tommy had hung from the bulletin board by a string, and he wrote "Play baseball in the park." Mr. L. came outside and added his own too, which was "Make up silly knock-knock jokes." Mom took a long time thinking about hers, but finally she put down "Be extra kind to the people you love," and then she gave me a kiss on the forehead.

We stayed there a long time, looking at the list, and watched while people came by and added things. And everyone had nice things to say about Jared.

When we were getting ready to leave, I went to find Tommy inside the store. He was opening up a package of Ding-Dongs.

"They got damaged," he told me.

I was starting to notice that when Tommy was around, it was only things made of chocolate that got damaged, but all I said was "Jared's birthday turned out pretty good, I think."

"Me too," he said. He held out the Ding-Dongs. "Want one?"

"Thanks." I grabbed one out of the package. "Well, see ya," I said.

"Hey, Annie?"

I turned around.

Tommy was looking down at his shoes. "I still miss Jared," he said.

"Yeah," I told him. "Me too."

"But . . . well, you're not too terrible to hang out with or anything."

I took another bite of Ding-Dong. "You're pretty okay too," I said.

twenty-four

●●●

When we got back home, there was a leaf stuck under the front door. And sure enough, when I checked the answering machine, there was a message from Rebecca.

"We're back from church!" It was all loud hollering. "Come on over as soon as you get this! I have to show you something important!"

I heaved Dr. Young's dictionary off my bookshelf so I could return it to him, and then I went to the garage and put on all my gear—helmet, elbow pads, kneepads, ankle bandages. Then I looked at my bike, sitting in the corner by Dad's car.

Walking would be the safest thing.

But biking would be quicker.

I dumped the dictionary in the front basket, took a deep deep breath, and swung my leg over my bicycle. And I headed down the street to Rebecca's.

Dr. Young answered the door. Before he could even say anything at all, I asked him a question.

"I don't have Ebola, do I?"

Dr. Young scratched his chin and thought about it. "Most likely not," he said.

"That's what I thought. Because some of the symptoms fit, but not most of them."

He looked at me, and it was a serious look but not the dead-brother one this time. This one was more gladness behind the eyes. "You know something, Annie? You could grow up to be a very good doctor one day."

And even though I'd never thought of that before, I sort of liked it. "Well"—I held out the dictionary—"anyway, I just wanted to give this back. Thanks for letting me borrow it."

"You're welcome. Did it come in handy?"

I nodded. "I found a word for your wall," I told him.

"Oh?"

"Yeah. Instead of that old one. *Despondent.* I found a better one." I pointed to where I'd marked it with a Post-it.

Dr. Young opened to the right page and scrolled his finger across the word I'd highlighted with purple marker. *"Radiant,"* he said, and then he looked up at me. "That's a good word, Annie."

"It's from a book," I told him. *"Charlotte's Web."* The dictionary said it could mean either "glowing brightly" or "emanating great joy, love, or health." "It's not . . ." I stuck my hands in my pockets and looked up at him. "I'm not sure I'm 'radiant' *yet,*" I said, "but maybe one day I will be."

"Annie," Dr. Young said, shutting the dictionary, "I think you are very close to radiant." And that might've been just about the nicest thing anyone ever told me.

Rebecca raced out onto the porch then, plowing

right into her dad in the doorway. "There you are!" she shouted. She was wearing her bike helmet. "Come on! We're going to Doug's!"

"Doug's?" I said as Rebecca yanked me off the porch. But she didn't explain, just hopped on her bike and motioned for me to follow her. We pedaled fast as cougars the whole way.

Doug was waiting for us when we got there, and he was wearing his bike helmet too, but he wasn't on his bike. He was standing in the middle of his yard, and there were pool noodles everywhere, sticking out of the ground like tent poles, and balanced between chairs, and hanging down from the branches of the elm tree.

"What happened to your yard?" I asked him.

"It's an obstacle course!" Rebecca hollered. "We made it!"

I whacked down my kickstand and put both my feet firm on the ground. "But I don't want to do an obstacle course," I said, and I hoped I was being extra glary at Doug while I said it. "I *told* you. Obstacle courses are—"

"It's not dangerous," Doug said. "Not this one. We got pillows." He pointed to a giant pile of them under the tree.

"And duct tape!" Rebecca shouted, pulling a roll out of her bike basket.

I took turns staring at both of them. They were acting nuttier than pecan pie. "Huh?"

"It's called pillow races," Doug told me. "Me and Rebecca made it up. So you could play."

"Yeah!" Rebecca nodded her head up and down all excited. "The rule is you can only race if you're wearing pillows! And bike helmets!"

"Well . . ." I looked around the yard, at all the pool noodles everywhere. It must've taken them forever to set it up. "What if I just watch you guys play?"

"Nope," Doug said, and he shook his head. "That's not how it works."

That's when Doug and Rebecca strapped the pillows to me with duct tape, one in front and one in back. Then they strapped pillows to each other, too.

And even though I felt stranger than a green

flamingo, I had to admit the obstacle course looked pretty fun.

"Okay!" Rebecca shouted, her arms poofed out to her sides because of the pillows. "I got the stopwatch! Annie goes first!"

"Where's the start?" I asked.

Doug punched himself twice in the belly where his pillow was, and it made a nice low thudding sound. "Over on the porch," he said. "You have to slide down two steps on your butt, and then you cross over to that chair"—he pointed—"and do a ninja leap. And then we'll tell you the rest as you go."

"Got it." I waddled over to the porch.

I had just plopped myself down on the second-to-last step when I felt something scrunch in the back pocket of my shorts. I wrestled my arm through the pillows until I reached my pocket, and I pulled the thing out.

It was a folded-up piece of paper with the word INDESTRUCTIBLE underlined three times.

"What's that!" Rebecca shouted from across the yard.

I looked at the paper in my hand for a second, and then I looked up at Rebecca and Doug, waiting for me under the elm tree like two giant grinning marshmallows. And then, without even thinking twice about it, I ripped my will in half.

"Nothing!" I shouted back.

"You ready?" Doug asked. Rebecca's thumb was hovering over the stopwatch.

"Yup!" I cried, dumping the pieces of my will on Doug's porch. "I'm gonna win, too! The slowest racer's a"—I tried to think of a really good word from the word wall—"rabble-rouser!"

Rebecca laughed at that. "Trundle bed!" she hollered.

"Halitosis!" I screeched.

"Needle-nose pliers!" Doug wailed.

Then Rebecca shouted at me that she was starting the timer, so I was *off*!

And somehow, while I was busy sliding and leaping and dancing and dodging, my brain managed to figure something out.

Maybe it only took one person to open an umbrella and stick it up in the air to block out the rain, but it took a whole lot of people to close it. And even though I was pretty sure I still had a few more inches to go, I knew that once my umbrella was all the way closed, I was going to keep it like that for a long time.

Because as it turned out, I sure did like the sunshine.

• • •

Many thanks are due to Dr. Daniel Danila and Dr. Patrick Kemper for their expert medical advice, and to Minna Balbas and Janine O'Malley for putting me in touch with them.

I owe countless cups of coffee to each of my fellow "Longstockings"—Kathryne Alfred, Coe Booth, Daphne Grab, Lisa Greenwald, Jenny Han, Caroline Hickey, and Siobhan Vivian—for their constant encouragement and brilliant advice. And I thank my lucky stars for Beth Potter and Salem Whalen, good friends with great ideas, and for Melissa Sassin, whose late-night pep talks proved even more effective than mint chip ice cream. Thanks to Dad, whose uncanny knowledge of obscure diseases finally came in handy, and to Mom, of course, for being Mom.

Last but not least, I am filled with gratitude for Stephen Barbara, who is almost certainly the world's best agent, and to the ever-patient Jill Santopolo, editor extraordinaire.